A Century of November

A Century of November

🐝

A Novel

W. D. WETHERELL

UNIVERSITY OF MICHIGAN PRESS

Ann Arbor

Copyright © by W. D. Wetherell 2004
Published in the United States of America by
The University of Michigan Press
Manufactured in the United States of America
♾ Printed on acid-free paper

2007   2006   2005   2004   4   3   2   1

*A CIP catalog record for this book is available
from the British Library.*

Library of Congress Cataloging-in-Publication Data

Wetherell, W. D., 1948–
A century of November : a novel / W.D. Wetherell.
     p.   cm. — (Michigan literary fiction awards)
ISBN 0-472-11431-X (acid-free paper)
I. Title. II. Series.
PS3573.E9248C46 2004
813'.54—dc22   2004007659

For Phil and Mary

A Century of November

HE JUDGED MEN AND HE GREW APPLES and it was a perilous autumn for both. A surprise autumn—the apples had promised so much. They blossomed early, luxuriously, with a rich pink-white color that went beyond anything he had ever seen. For once there was no late snow, no storm whipping in from the Pacific, no frost. In June, he was already ordering extra crates from a dealer in Vancouver, carving crutches to support the fruit-heavy limbs. In July, smoke blew across the strait from fires on the mainland, acrid and sticky, not like wood burning at all, but something more malignant. With no young men to fight them, the fires continued all summer, until each apple tree in the orchard was doubled by a spiky silhouette of gray. From Flanders, local people said, shaking their heads. They were convinced it wasn't forest fires at all, but mustard gas blown all the way from France. By September, the apples were scabbed with yellow and orange rust, and now, here in late October, there was nothing hanging on the branches but pitted little sacks of empty brown flesh.

As for men, there wasn't much to say. His job as magistrate had never been easier. For three years now there had hardly been a crime worth mentioning, even though the town was only a few years removed from being frontier. There were drunken Indians, there were the bastards who sold it to them, the fishermen down on their luck who smuggled hooch in from the States, but except for those, the entire island had been well-behaved right through the duration. It was as if the evil in the world had turned liquid, spun sideways in a whirlpool, spewed all its fury toward France as part of the same desperate cycle that returned the smoke to them.

He was magistrate because he was the only person on that part of the coast who could be magistrate—a stipendiary magistrate devoted to, in the words of his oath, *insuring the equal rights of the poor and the rich, after his cunning, wit and power.* In normal times, this was no easy task. He had been shot at once. Shot at from ambush doing what he was doing now, strolling up the long rows of the orchard appraising how things stood. It had been spring then. The shot clipped a branch directly above him, covering him in a shower of white petals. "Missed," he remembered thinking, as the report echoed across the headlands and the petals tickled his face. He had been blind that way, stupid. *Missed.*

The tree, the fractured branch, became a shrine for him, a place he went to whenever he took the judging too seriously or not seriously enough. And now it was something more than that, his lucky spot, a sanctuary, the one place in the world he could stand and be safe. The bullet wound seemed to release something vital in the tree, since it was the only one in that row that managed a fully formed apple. A joke of course—he knew when fate waxed sardonic, having seen it so often from the bench. He reached to touch it now. Its skin was wet and slippery from the early rain, but the old familiar heft of it, the oval fullness, felt good against his palm.

He was standing there, his hands plunged again in his jacket pockets, his collar turned against the wind, when he saw something move across and briefly darken the narrow view of the water the orchard commanded. Someone walking up from the beach, which meant someone who had come by boat. He felt a premonition seeing that. He felt a premonition because at no time in the last two years had anyone approached him across any separation of any size without his feeling a premonition. But perhaps this wasn't the right word. It went deeper than that. It was certainty, one that hardened as the shape grew closer and he recognized who it was.

Ira Cooper. Short, stubby, solid, walking in the peculiarly clumsy way he favored, as if there were a sack of bricks looped over his shoulders. He picked his way up the grassy hill, his black sea boots like huge blunt plows gouging out the steps. He came, Marden noticed, precisely along the path the bullet had traveled years ago. Up the hill, through the orchard gate, along the longest row toward the wounded branch.

It was Cooper who had brought the news of Laura's death three weeks earlier. She had been visiting her sister in Vancouver. A long visit, all of August and deep into autumn, for reasons Marden didn't fully understand. The strain of worrying about Billy. The isolation of the island, the fact she needed more life, more urgency, than what could be found there. The difference in their ages. Something new and dark in him. There were reasons, lots of reasons, but none that solved the mystery. The important thing was that she planned on coming back. He had a long, loving letter from her giving the boat she was crossing on, the time of her arrival.

The storm hit the day she was supposed to leave, and lasted for a full week, sending the barometer plunging, tossing up williwaws, wiping all shipping off the strait. With extra time, she had done something characteristic: gone to a hospital outside the city to visit a friend of Billy's, a corporal in the same regiment, who had been invalided home due to wounds. He was coughing when she visited him, felt weak in a way the doctors couldn't account for. Within twenty-four hours he had died of what they finally decided was pneumatic influenza.

Her turn came next, her turn like so many. Perfectly fit on Monday, she felt feverish on Tuesday, and by Thursday she was dead. The Spanish flu. It had a name now, an identity, and the papers talked of nothing else, not even the war. Cooper had brought the news over— and now here he was climbing the hill again with the same weight around his shoulders, the same heavy and reluctant gait.

Death could choose no better messenger. There was so much homeliness in his sun-scarred face, so much sincerity in his bashful expression, so much strength spread so evenly across his body, that it was impossible to imagine him being the agent for anything but the hardest truth. Their friendship went back nearly three decades, to the time when Marden first came to Vancouver Island from Montreal, already in love with the west, determined to grow with it toward whatever destiny it was headed for. Cooper, born in Campbell River to a gold miner and his Tlingit wife, had taken him under his wing. They had trolled salmon together, prospected, worked in the woods, beachcombed, even done their bit of smuggling. Both were quiet men. If anything, they grew even quieter in each other's presence, learning to decipher what was on the other's mind by the way they held their shoulders, gripped a boat's wheel, peered into the weather.

And so, even before Cooper was fully up to him, Marden had read what was in his posture. Cooper, ducking to get under a branch, tried walking straighter, as if to soften his message, but he was too short and squat to pull this off. He stooped, looked Marden in the eye, nodded. And because it was impossible not to, Marden asked him the question he always asked when seeing him after any absence, ever since he could remember.

"How's the water, Coop?"

Cooper grimaced—it was a grimace that could frighten children from fifty yards away. "Smooth," he said, his voice hoarse around the word. "Too smooth. You know how it gets."

He reached into his pocket, pulled out the letter Marden already knew must be there. It was a yellow envelope—not the bright yellow a friend or lover might send, but an ugly manila shade that could only be official.

"Came across on the packet," Cooper said, handing it over. "Margaret took it at the store. She lowered the flag to let me know it was important. I came in to the cove

and there she was holding it. That's what happened—"
He made his face uglier. "Until now."

Marden opened the envelope, unfolded the letter, read it quickly, the few key phrases. *Your son Corporal William C. Marden Princess Alexandra's Canadian Light Infantry . . . in the advance past Gheluvelt on 10 Oct . . . a great favorite in the regiment and was going on so well . . . a true son of Canada typifying all the best in our dominion . . . our deepest regrets . . . R. C. H. Vickers Colonel commanding.*

The words, most of them, hardly made any impression on the stupor that had taken hold of him since Laura's death. He was armored in that respect, padded in numbness. And yet there was a chink, one the letter found immediately, the one word that could penetrate, damage, burn. *Gheluvelt.* He stared at it again, the odd form it made on the paper, the mocking way it lay there, offering no easy logic for the tongue, no familiar pattern for the eye, barbarous in that respect, unseemly, crude. *Gheluvelt.* He knew the moment he saw it that of all the words he had ever used in his life, all the words he had read, uttered, heard or seen, this one alone really mattered. It burned itself in. He felt it branded on his wrist, on his arm, on his forehead. *Gheluvelt.*

And he knew in that same instant that he was wrong about that long-ago shot having missed, the one fired at him from ambush by the disgruntled logger or the aggrieved plaintiff or the wife beater with a grudge. It had hit a branch, true, but without his realizing it the bullet must have split in two, the halves separating, flying eastward waiting to hit something solid before ricocheting back to the orchard again, this time straight for his heart.

Laura was first. Not hard tracing the course of that bullet. The semi-detached house in the quiet Vancouver street, the curtains suddenly drawn, the doctor's grim head shake, Kathy, his sister-in-law, going to the telephone to call her husband, Roger, the man who would know what to do. The argument about how best to send him the news, the impossibility of telephoning, the coldness of a wire, someone finally remembering that Ira Cooper was in town taking delivery of a new boat— and thus the bullet, the first half, coming across with him, a man in black oilskins bearing sad news for a friend.

A bullet splits apart on an apple branch. One ricochet is short and brutally comprehensible, but the other is much longer, extending across half the world, a trajectory almost impossible for him to imagine. Gheluvelt— but what did that mean? When he tried to get his mind around it all he found was a model Belgian village, cottages with thatched roofs ringed by a trench like the ones drawn in the newspapers, with plank fire steps, wire revetting, plump sandbags, something that looked inviting, sheltering, warm. He knew it couldn't be anything like that, the village would have to be chopped into cubes, and muddied and thrown all to chaos, but that wasn't an image that came easily to a man like him.

Gheluvelt, that was the impossible part, his mind couldn't reach it, but then the trajectory grew straighter. There would be the stretcher bearer who found him, or maybe a pal. They would bring the news back to the trench, report to the sergeant, the commanding officer, formally at roll call, informally before that—a rumor at first, then a verified fact. From there the news would go back to brigade headquarters, the colonel in charge. He would write something official, an entry in a hideous ledger, then the personal note, written to one of three or four prescribed forms.

And then? How did mail proceed across Flanders? By train, via courier, an enormous sack thrown on a lorry or dumped on a train? Back to Calais or another of the Channel ports, over to Dover or Folkestone, by rail to London, the Dominions office, Canada House, a bureaucrat whose job it was to guide the bullets toward the hearts meant to receive them. From London to Liverpool, then onto an empty transport for the voyage back to Halifax, to be put on another train, through the Maritimes to Montreal and onto another train to make the long journey west . . . all the way back to Cooper again, bearing his second message, the bullet's missing half, seven days in the passage, plowing home next to the jagged entry hole left by the first one.

Cooper. He had walked off a decent distance, stood under a branch with his hands clasped behind his back, frowning at the withered apples, as if withered apples were the world's only problem. He came back now, applied the same pensive frown to the ground, then suddenly glanced up to stare him straight in the eyes.

"Look here, Charles. There's nothing for you on the island now. The boat's down below. I could take you over."

If in that moment Cooper had proposed flying to Mars together, Marden would have assented—he was open to the first push that came along. It was madness to be alone. Madness. Whatever else the letter implied, it required motion of some kind, motion for its own sake, anything to shake free of the stupor, the helplessness, that he knew would become permanent if he didn't move at once.

There were no practical difficulties. Parker down in Belloy River could handle any cases that came along. The orchard, the apples that under ordinary circumstances he could never leave until picking, consisted of shrunken little sacks that could drop off on their own.

Vancouver made sense for many reasons. There were friends there, officials who could give him information on precisely what had happened, a depot the regiment maintained, friends of Billy who might be able to add their own stories. Noise, bustle, the press of strangers—hadn't that been the tonic Laura craved? A few days there and he could begin to come to terms with things. Vancouver made sense.

Cooper stood waiting for an answer, his blocky chin screwed up toward his blocky forehead, so it was like looking at an anchor with eyes. Marden nodded—and then the two men were walking single-file back toward the house, Marden to throw some clothes into his traveling bag, Cooper to go around shuttering the windows in case there was a blow.

Finishing, he went down to the landing to ready the boat, leaving Marden to follow. He did, but not straight away. There was a confused moment by Laura's grave there under the tallest, darkest spruce, then a last glance back at the dying orchard, the withered fruit looking, from that distance, like Christmas ornaments singed in a fire . . . and then he was onto the gravel path that crested the headland and tipped toward the beach, walking fast to keep up with the grade, then faster, running now, running as hard and desperately as a boy.

II

Cooper hadn't been exaggerating about the sea's stillness. Marden would always remember how calm it was that night, what ripples there were on the water smoothing themselves out with the sunset, turning indigo, then purple so it was as if the bow of Cooper's boat plowed silk. A sculling oar would have gotten them across to the mainland, it was so still. For long minutes, Cooper, caught up in the same mood he was, would turn the engine off just to see how far they could glide.

The boils that usually troubled these waters, the whirlpools, lay weak and quiescent. The surface was covered with a lazy scum of broken starfish arms, old anemone tubercles, severed flatworms, shredded kelp. Chaos underneath, conflict, turmoil—and yet on the surface, a perfection that mirrored stars.

Neither man said a word during the passage. Cooper stood behind the wheel, lost in steering; Marden sat a little behind him on an old camp stool, looking now toward the island, now toward the mainland, sipping on a mug of tea that had long since turned cold. They were far enough out that he could see the mountains behind Nanimo, the matching peaks on the mainland, both ranges holding enough iridescence to their snow to stand out against the dark. It was a middle passage

Cooper took down the strait. It was a middle passage Marden needed, with those high walls on either side shunting his thoughts so they couldn't stray too far one way or the other.

A landscape that he loved. A landscape that, not for the first time in his life there, suggested a way he might conduct himself, a manner of being. He couldn't articulate to himself what this might be, not at first, but he had plenty of time to puzzle it out. The crossing took most of the night. There were times when Cooper was so silent, the sea so quiet, that Marden felt as if he were flying weightless over the water, levitated, and it was only the hard remembrance of the letter that brought him back down.

The voyage was not without incident. A killer whale surfaced off to starboard, with a pungent, earthy smell that seemed at odds with its ghostly up and down. Later, the calm was disturbed by a heavy churn that came athwart them and nearly rolled them over—the wake of a destroyer or corvette coming into Vancouver twenty miles away, with nothing to stop its outspreading chevrons until they met Cooper's hull. Toward dawn sea birds began following them, expecting bait. The sun, in rising, flashed first off Marden's copper tea mug, though now the dregs in it were frozen.

No matter. By then his resolution had formed. The steep walls of mountains, the deep passage between walls. Could a man conduct himself that way, not forever, but for as long as it took to steer clear? The walls represented thinking, feeling, judging. Could a man go a month in a middle passage without thinking or feeling or judging at all? He would see the world, observe it, but make no judgements of any kind, not until he passed through the strait to the place he needed to see, *must* see, and then he would judge all he damned well pleased.

That was part of it. The other part came with the hum of the engine deep within the deck, the soothing throb it left in his toes and heels, the matching sensation that came with gliding effortlessly through the water. If the mountains suggested an attitude, a way of thinking—a way of *not* thinking—then the motion suggested where he might find solace, enough to get him through the passage and temporarily serve in the place of thought.

Even then, coming this far with it, he still couldn't put his resolution into words. It was the reason he said nothing to Cooper. Now that it was light out they had no trouble talking with each other, but it was about the boats standing in toward the mainland, the buoys, the trawlers, many owned by men they knew. Marden, talking softly so Cooper wouldn't argue, asked to be dropped off at Gibsons where he could take the ferry the short distance into the city. Vancouver harbor would be full of navy ships, patrol boats, torpedo nets, and he didn't want Cooper bothered.

They were near enough the mainland to see the ferry waiting with a head of steam. Cooper tugged the wheel to starboard in protest, but in the end he stood in toward the pier. They shook hands on the gangway. The deckhands were already tossing the ropes down from the bollards, so they didn't have much time.

"I'll meet you here in three days," Cooper said, making it partly a question, partly a command. "Eight o'clock, unless there's weather."

For the first time in their friendship, Marden felt

unable to meet his eyes. Cooper was too bothered to notice. He crossed within touching distance of the ferry's hull, stood staring up at the rose insignia that was rusty and blistered, ready to flake off—stood there staring, then spat bitterly toward the water.

"The war won't end, you know that, Charles? Not next year, not in 1920 either, and by then all the weapons will be worse. Jack turns eighteen in March. I'm not letting him be taken. I'm going to hide him up in the mountains—I've the spot all picked out. I've talked it over with Margaret and she's with me strong."

A year ago Cooper had been as rabid a patriot as there was on the coast—he had mounted a high-powered rifle in the bow of his boat, in the event one of the Kaiser's submarines had made it to the Pacific. Marden himself, though he was proud of the Canadian regiments in a way that nearly choked him, had seen too much of sudden death to be rabid in that way. He had gotten this far in the war by telling himself he had no illusions about what it was like. He thought Billy would be protected by that, having a father with no illusions. But that, of course, had been his biggest illusion.

"I'm with you, too, Coop," he said. He wanted to hug him, hug him hard, but the ferry whistle was blowing now and a hunchbacked, red-eared Cooper was already stomping off across the pier.

III

It was two hours to Vancouver. The ferry had its own kind of throb, deeper than the fishing boats, grittier, yet

13

part of the same subterranean current that drove him on. He stood on deck, cold as it was, keeping the mountains in sight as long as possible. There were few other passengers. The ferry stopped at every ramshackle pier and abandoned cannery between Gibsons and North Vancouver, but only at one of them did anyone get on.

He was only a little older than Marden was himself, in his fifties at most, dressed impeccably in a black overcoat with a silk collar, making it seem he was going, not into work in the city, but to the opera or a ball. Seeing the ferry approach, a bit late for it, he walked calmly down the path along a stream that emptied into the strait. Marden couldn't help admiring him, this sauntering man. Yes, that was the way to hold yourself during an autumn like this one. Aloof, proud, insulated within your dignity from anyone's prying stares.

Reaching Vancouver, they were quickly caught up in the harbor's shipping. The dignified man walked around the deck in order to be first down the gangway. By the time Marden started down he was already standing below on the pier, guiding a porter to his one small trunk. The trunk delivered, the porter tipped, the man did something odd. He reached into the pocket of his overcoat, unfolded something that looked like an oversized handkerchief, shook it fully open, then carefully, with the same economy of motion, tied it in a bandanna over his face.

A bank robber—a gentleman bank robber. Marden, curious, kept his eye on him, even began following him through the streets. A block in from the pier came a street cleaner with a similar bandanna over his mouth, then a woman pushing a perambulator, mother and child with matching masks made out of a soft, gingham-like material, and then he was past the last of the wharf buildings out into an open square full of grunting steve-dores, shouting taxi drivers, Chinese peddlers, all of them wearing these same wretched masks.

The influenza had taken hold, the plague. Three blocks in from the waterfront the entire city seemed deserted, what few people were about looking at him with suspicion and fear. Stores were shuttered—signs explained their owners had gone on vacation. He meant to take a tram, but he couldn't find one running—most had been abandoned by their drivers in the middle of the tracks. Gangs of prisoners tossed pails of disinfectant over the pavement, then stood talking quietly with their hands cupped over their mouths like they were hoarding cigarettes. A deserted theatre advertised Charlie Chaplin. Someone had taken a pencil and sketched in a mask over Chaplin's face.

He was halfway to his sister-in-law's, walking in the center of the deserted avenue, when he heard a sharp metallic pounding. It was a squad of soldiers marching three abreast—he had to step to the side to make room. They were splendid-looking boys, young and fit, puttees wrapped like strong khaki springs around their legs. Even the gauze over their mouths couldn't hide the fact many were smiling. Young boys like Billy was young. Young boys like Billy.

He was waiting for them to pass when there came a loud cackling noise right behind him. It was a wizened little man with a flat cloth hat slouched down over a sar-donic expression. He didn't wear a mask—his face seemed to blaze in stubbled whiteness.

"Rats," he said, making his voice cackle again. "Rats!"

He waited until the first rank of soldiers passed, then pointed again. "On their backs, mister. Look what's on their backs!"

Each soldier carried a burlap sack—each sack bulged toward the bottom, some with two lumps, some with three.

"They're drowning them! Throwing them in the harbor! Soldiers against rats! Soldiers against rats!"

He yelled it loud enough that the soldiers heard him. One turned and waved, another gave him a good-natured finger. They marched on past at the double quick, barked at by their sergeant. When Marden turned around again, the wizened little man was gone.

The city seemed emptier, colder, once the soldiers left, with the smell of smoldering coal fires being the only sign of life. He was up to Clarence Street now, his last chance to turn aside. Toward the left was Kathy's house, the garden with her prize-winning roses, a room overlooking the water, sympathetic listeners, friends, the connections that would begin to make sense of things. To his left was the rational, considered way to go. But even after walking that far atop dead pavement, the current he had felt beneath Cooper's boat still carried him, and left was not the direction it wanted him to turn.

The Canadian Pacific station was even more crowded than the ferry dock had been, with long queues before every ticket window. People fleeing—the lucky ones with definite places to go. Outside on the plaza a piano had fallen from a lorry and exploded across the road. Families, including the first children he had seen, stood there staring at the shattered insides as they waited in line.

"Yes, sir?" the ticket agent said, when it came his turn.

Marden hesitated, enough so the agent looked up.

"Would you like a ticket then, sir?"

"Halifax."

"Halifax? Yes, sir, a sleeper?"

"A sleeper. Yes, fine."

He asked about the boarding time, then edged his way through the crowd to a newspaper stand, hoping to find something that would hold his attention. There was nothing except the usual. Books about the war with jingoistic titles, or the local papers, the sober ones with headlines announcing new quarantine measures, the popular ones, in bolder headlines, announcing the worst was past.

It was more than he could do to buy any of these. Instead, he reached high on the rack for a small leather diary, thumbed through it quickly, then counted out the proper coins. He had never kept a diary before, but perhaps it would help shorten the journey. He wouldn't use it to record his thoughts—his thoughts were something he was expressly shutting out—but to keep a simple log of the route, the towns, the distances. Put these down, keep it faithfully, and it might help prevent what he feared most—judging, judging precipitously, judging before he got there, saw it with his own eyes, the very spot.

The train left on schedule—his sleeper was the very last car. He had thrown his bag up in the rack, settled down against the window, when he saw a cloud shoot past the glass. It wasn't normal steam. It turned dark, made itself into a fist, drummed so hard against the side of the train that the window bulged inward. Men appeared, standing on the platform with gas masks over their faces, carrying heavy metal canisters that made their knees sag. The fog swelled them to twice their normal size. They lumbered about like giants, aiming disinfectant toward the cars through pressurized nozzles, as if not only to blast the train and its occupants all the way across the continent, but to permanently blind them as well.

Whatever they used was sticky and plaster-like—it wasn't until the first mountains that the cold against the window peeled it off. By then it was nearly dark. The porter came through the car with his gong, announcing dinner, but Marden stayed where he was. Back in the west, visible only on the long southward curves, was an amber keyhole of sunlight. He could picture what it must be like in the orchard, knew the effect well. The crepuscular light slanting down from the clouds in graphite-colored shafts, burning circles on the water, flashing a few last seconds of gladness before fading out. He could sense that through the window, caught it one last time before the dark thickened into a tunnel—and then the moment was over, and with all that happened on his journey, he never looked toward the west again until its very end.

IV

They were three days crossing the continent. At first, in the mountains, there was no sign of war. Winter had clamped down hard here—for long miles the train's reflection was mirrored by icy blue cliffs. Twice they were stopped by avalanches, had to wait on a siding until the plows did their job. In every tunnel would come a sharp rattling sound as stalactites of ice were sliced by the engine's hood.

Descending onto the prairies was like emerging into spring. The stubble from the wheat harvest was just green enough to suggest living grass, and the sun that had been constricted by the mountain passes now had room to broaden and stretch. Still, it was bitter enough, the times the train stopped for water and they were allowed to walk along the tracks. One time up to the engine and back was all Marden could manage, even with his duffel coat buttoned tight against the wind. At each of these stops children would appear from God knows where, selling wrinkled old berries or wreaths woven out of buffalo grass. Marden always bought whatever they proffered. He tried talking with them, but it was like talking to the wind, they were so shy, so liable to take flight. They raced the train as it gained speed, the boys and girls both, mouths open, legs pumping, coats spreading apart like wings.

There were cities, too, though they always passed through them at night, so they were nothing more than blurred impressions. Calgary a string of frightened ponies being herded somewhere by spotlights. Regina hidden by a snow squall. A cigar-like pall enveloping Winnipeg. Always when daylight returned they would be back out on the prairies, with nothing visible on the horizon except bright red grain elevators, yellow church steeples, the corrugated shimmer left in emptiness by the wind.

Each lonely town had its own station; at each, several people would be waiting as the train pulled in. Most of these were women wrapped in heavy black coats, carrying hampers so they could save money on food, often seen off by friends who formed a ring around them on the platform as if to protect them from the cold. Even so, there was a windblown effect in all of them. Their faces were red, their postures stooped, making it seem the wind had scoured the land, tested it, and these women were what had blown loose first.

At one station a group of farm boys was shepherded in by a recruiting sergeant who, once he had them seated, had the sense to leave them alone. They acted self-conscious at first, serious, bashful, but this soon wore off. Their natural high spirits took over, and all through the night Marden could hear their laughter as they played their endless hands of cards.

🐂

Marden kept to himself, talked only when he had to, skipped many meals. This wasn't because he needed to choke back on his emotions—there was little emotion now to choke back. Laura had always chided him about his famous self-control, a criticism he never understood, since all he could remember were times on the bench trying unsuccessfully to do just that—to keep his emotions in check in cases he cared so much about it was all he could do not to scream at man's stupidity or cry with pity at his self-inflicted pain.

On the train all that seemed very distant. It was as if his emotions had dried up completely, the energy that usually went into them having been transferred to his eyes. He couldn't get enough of the window. He sat there for hours at a stretch with his face pressed against the glass, seeing in a way he had never seen before—farther in a literal sense than he had ever managed, while below that, deeper, he couldn't see anything at all.

Toward the end of the second day, when it had grown too dark for the window, he remembered the diary he had purchased back in Vancouver. He fetched it from his bag, sat down with it balanced across one knee, pulled out a stubby pencil, started writing before he had time to become self-conscious.

Halfway point today, so the conductor said. Scruffy country, not quite woods. An apple orchard. Porters, Wolf Rivers, no fruit. The recruits must have smuggled aboard some liquor, since all acted lethargic this morning, chastened. Has it occurred to them yet what they're in for? Had a surprise this afternoon. Passed in the aisle the man I saw back on the Vancouver ferry, the gent in formal clothes, the one who donned the bandanna. Not wearing it now, but a black armband around his jacket sleeve. Recognized me I think. A curt little nod. Nearing Lake of the Woods, first real trees in a thousand miles. Out the window in the early twilight, walking along the cinders, a wolf with a white beard of ice.

In this desert of emotion, these cold rigid tracks, two images of Billy were strong enough to burst through. The first came while they were still in the Rockies, coming down the long pass that ended near Banff. The summer before the war, when he was still only sixteen, Billy took a job with the forestry people as fire lookout on Mount Kennet. It had been a hard job, a lonely one, but even at sixteen there was a self-sufficient reliability to him that made people want to trust him with the most difficult tasks. Later that summer he had joined a survey party exploring the unclimbed Rockies peaks. He had been taken on as a packer, but then toward the end he had worked his way up to being a member of the climbing party, the ones who struck out for the summits.

That was the first image, the photograph taken on one of the peaks—tanned, fit, proud, a happy smile across his absurdly young face, his blond hair ragged from a backwoods haircut, his eyes wide the way they got when he was about to crack a joke . . . a thick hemp rope bulging around his chest like an extra heart, an ice axe cocked over his shoulder like a gun.

The other image was vaguer, harder to focus on. Outside Toronto, passing a quiet suburban station, he saw a young girl standing alone on the platform waiting for a local train. She was pensive-looking, demure—her hands were folded neatly in front of her around a small white purse, and the collar of her coat touched the bottom of her short auburn hair. Just a glimpse—in an instant a freight train swept past blocking the view—

and yet it was enough to make Marden remember the last letter Billy had sent home.

He hadn't written many letters, three or four in two years. Always, when he and Laura read them out loud to each other, they'd gotten the feeling he wasn't chary with words because he had none, but because he overflowed with too many, didn't know where to start.

This last letter, for him, had been almost chatty. *We're in billets in Wiltshire,* he wrote. *The local people have been wonderfully kind. Wonderfully. I walked with a girl along a country lane there. I told her about the island. It was good, it brought everything back to me. She liked especially the stories about Uncle Coop and his pet bear. We're for France tomorrow, the entire regiment. Will write soon. Your loving son William.*

The words came back to him now, with the sight of the girl. He tried holding it sharp in his imagination, an image of country lanes and summer verdancy and pensive young girls. He hoped she had been kind. For Billy's sake, he hoped that more than anything.

❧

The good weather that pushed them across the continent disappeared along Lake Superior. Gales set in, blowing westward over open water. Nail-hard spray hit the side of the train and made it shudder—waves crested over the locomotive the way waves break over ships. Past Thunder Bay, running along the lake's edge, they were literally stopped in their tracks, and no progress was possible until another, more powerful locomotive was added to the front. Thirty years ago, a young man running away from home, heading west for the first time, he hadn't felt free until this very spot, the long northern shore of Superior, the shield, with its majesty, loneliness, expanse. Now here he was coming back east again—and here the lake was, spinning in fury, telling him not to.

He began seeing the man from the ferry more often now. An observation car was attached to the coaches; the man could often be found standing near one end, staring out a porthole-sized window, smoking a cigarette in a long ivory holder, his hand, his right hand, adjusting and readjusting the black armband around his left arm. Up close, he resembled King Edward without the beard. There was something regal about him, dignified, though, from the vacancy in his eyes, it was obvious he carried a great burden.

Carrying the burden well, that was what struck Marden. Again, he felt the need to emulate him, as if this man were leading the way into grief, demonstrating how to compose your expression, the muscles of your face—how to enter it properly, giving in to it and yet not giving in. It was a valuable lesson. It was a bond between them. Only once did it result in an exchange of words.

This was during the worst of the storm. They had been stopped by water over the tracks, a long delay, and they had just resumed speed again, with the conductor going around assuring everyone they were still on schedule. The lights were slow in coming back on—there was a stuttered flash, darkness, then a burst of yellow that brought cheers from everyone in the coach. Marden, feeling chilled, was walking back to the dining car to find some coffee, when he came upon the man standing by the heavy metal door that led between cars. He was dressed in his overcoat, though no station was near, and at first Marden assumed it was because he felt chilled, too.

Marden was up to him—he was readying himself for the brief little nod they invariably exchanged—when something in the man's expression made him stop. All the dignity, the calm acceptance, was gone. His facial muscles, his very cheekbones, seemed to have slid down toward his chin, which was quivering. Whatever was stoic in him had been cut with a knife. Marden saw this so clearly, with such force, that it was impossible not to speak.

"I'm sorry."

The man looked sharply up at him, seemed startled, then dumbly nodded up and down.

"Where?" Marden asked.

"Vimy Ridge," the man said, his voice barely above a whisper. "A sniper's bullet. Quick."

"How old?"

"Eighteen." He stared past Marden's shoulder toward the window, severing the momentary connection between their eyes. "Very quick."

The man raised his arm in a blocking motion, then hurried past Marden up the car. The door opened at the far end—there was someone shouting—then the train braked with a sudden lurch that made Marden grab onto a seat to keep from falling down.

"Flooded again!" one of the recruits merrily shouted—but this was not why the train had stopped. Conductors rushed past, people began pointing out the windows, wiping their sleeves on the steamy glass, leaning over each other to see. Marden got to the door before anyone else, saw what was draped neatly over the iron handle: the man's elegant overcoat, dark and warm-looking, like a pelt that had been discarded because, in the end, it wasn't warm enough.

🐂

His suicide was the talk of the train, at least until Montreal, after which so many new passengers boarded it was soon forgotten. As before, most of these passengers were women, younger than the prairie women, more sophisticated, their black dresses shaped close to their figures, but their faces just as solemn and sad.

Of Montreal, he only had a brief glimpse before the dark came on. The bulk of the mountain, cathedral spires, the flat iron sheet of the St. Lawrence. None of this stirred anything in him, there were few flashes of recollection. His father's failures, his mother's grim scraping. Nothing could ever coat these with nostalgia. He felt truly numb now—there was no need to pretend—and the diary was the only thing that helped even a little.

New Brunswick. Spruce forests, mill towns, weirs. A tidy country compared to home. Potato fields turned over for winter. A lonely soldier guarding a bridge waves his rifle. Feeling the need for a woman next to me. No, not that. A deeper need. The way I desire Billy, his presence against me, pressing on the same muscles, the same indents on those muscles his body would make nestled against mine when he was small. The feeling his muscles were my muscles. Not in a proprietary way. No. But that strengthening, thickening, finding tautness, they would someday carry what I could no longer carry myself. A sign on a barn advertising codfish oil—my first glimpse of Nova Scotia. Arrived Halifax 8:37 P.M.

It was too late, he felt too tired, to do much searching. There was a boardinghouse near the station and this was where he spent the night, in a room with religious pictures on the walls, rubber sheets on the bed, and, wafting down the corridor, the fake moans of whores.

v

Two strong currents flowed in Halifax, and it was only gradually he began understanding they might form one. The first was the current, the impulse, that had been in him ever since crossing the strait in Cooper's thirty-footer. It was stronger on this side of the continent than it had been on the other, though stalled by the unexpected difficulties he faced, so it curled back on itself, became temporarily an eddy. The larger current was formed by the huge mass of people he saw on the streets—soldiers, sailors, merchantmen, civilians, people of every description, nationality and age, moving randomly within some purpose that was the exact opposite of random. What that impulse sprang from he was slow in understanding, just as he was slow in recognizing that his own motivation, the one he still thought of as personal and private, unique to him, had anything to do with the larger. And yet the immediate goal of all this striving was easy to identify: to end up at the harbor and board a waiting ship.

Like all large harbors he had experience of, Halifax's seemed determined to hide the fact it contained any water. There were warehouses and cranes and dry docks, and past these it was difficult to see. Even the ships seemed to act as walls. They were warehouse-sized, the convoy ships, and the only thing that differentiated them from the other buildings was that their sides were rustier, in more need of repair, as if they had been nibbled and snapped at by the Atlantic. Their guns, half hidden by tarpaulins, looked thinner than saw logs and not nearly as dangerous.

The crowds swarmed so thickly in front of the passenger terminals that Mounties rode along the edges keeping everyone in line. Marden found the Cunard office, joined the long queue extending from the booking counter out across Pier Two. He was standing there, looking, surely, as hopeless as he felt, when a quick narrow blade of a man detached himself from the crowd and hurried over.

"Morning, sir," he said, tipping his cap.

A pimp by the look of him—Marden readied himself for the sales pitch. For all his thinness, he had a boyish face that looked cut out of dough, his features pressed flat into the batter by his own thumb, a thumb which kept jerking up to swipe at his nose. What did they call themselves here? Haligonians? A spectral enough name for such a man.

He smiled, seeing Marden grimace. His manner combined the maximum deference with the maximum contempt.

"Lost a son, have we now? Going over to find communion with the soul of a freshly departed? Lots here in that position, sir. Lots going to France—if they can book a passage. Hardly a prayer, just look around you, sir. A thousand vying for a dozen berths. Even if they do manage a crossing, hardly likely old Jerry will stop the war for their convenience."

He laughed at this, his own ironic humor. But it was breathtaking, the directness. Was his own expression so easy to read that even the details were plain? Marden looked at him a little closer.

"How much?"

The man swiped at his nose again, but this time it escaped him and popped out on its own. "What the gent tells you there," he said, pointing to the ticket window. "Only triple."

For all the vileness in his manner, there was something clean and simple about the man. Money, the easiest transaction to understand.

"A cheque is all I have."

"Bank of Canada, sir? That would be fine then. Only I've been tallying and counting and I see now I was wrong in my figure. Four times the normal sum will do it. Not normal times, are they, sir? So many hands to wet if you catch my meaning. Eleven in the morning according to our reliable clock over there. You come back in three hours time and I'll be standing here or you ask anyone for Jimmy Bassett and I'll have your ticket. And which side would that be, sir? They say port is best when U-boats come in. Port I'll make it for the extra hundred."

❧

He spent his three hours on the hill near the Citadel, sitting on a marble bench staring out across the wide basin of the harbor. He had climbed high for a definite purpose. The infamous explosion. The munitions ship, the *Mount Blanc,* that had exploded mid-channel after a collision. The biggest man-caused explosion in the history of the world. Rumors had raced west well ahead of the official denials, but now that it was no secret, a year in the past, he wanted to appraise the damage for himself.

Once, working in the woods as a young man, he had come upon a section of forest where a meteorite had hit thirty years earlier when there were few white men on the coast. Trees were down in every direction, as jackstraws in a circular ring, their bark turned a bronze color as if everything had been petrified. Much the same effect could be seen here, though the damage was in torn houses, downed telegraph poles, fallen church steeples, twisted tram lines, collapsed chimneys. Three crescent lines of destruction could be traced in from the harbor toward the North End, forming an overlapping terrace where debris from one ring spilled across the next. Whole banks of earth had been torn away, so there were great parts of the city that looked as if they had been blasted back into granite, shorn of ornament, shaved.

Nothing moved within all this, no one was attempting to clean anything away. The breeze carried an iodine smell in from the ocean, though it was quickly smothered by the boiling malt smell from the surviving breweries. Gulls hovered over the wreckage, dipped, soared—a raven slanted down, like a stubby black pointer showing where to look. The dead had long since been buried, of course. What the scene suggested was that mourning, deep mourning, was still so intense no one could bear to do anything with the ruins but leave them exposed to whatever healing power came down from the sun. He was used to considering death as something that happened to one person at a time, and now here, four thousand miles from the front line, was evidence of a different style of death, death all together, death en masse, and he realized that whatever else happened during his journey he would have to change his calculations, brutalize his calculations, accordingly.

He spent his three hours there, taking this in. When he got back to Pier Two, Jimmy Bassett was waiting right where he had promised, an orange ticket flapping in his hand like a patriotic flag.

"Perfectly valid, sir, as you'll find when you hand it over. I obtained the port side, and above the waterline, so I added in the extra tariff. All women booked besides you, that's what they tell me. War widows going over to the cemeteries. I'd be careful if I were you, sir. Widows can eat a man up—him who's lucky!"

VI

ULTONIA, he wrote, taking up the diary again, printing the word in the formal block letters it deserved. Cunarder. A decent enough ship. Camouflaged—vast sweeps of black, gray and white. En route from New York to Southampton via Halifax. No convoy—we're said to be too fast for a submarine to catch. Former troopship. Every inch of plating scratched with soldiers' initials, regiment, home town. My smooth-talking friend didn't come through with the cabin he promised.

9C. Starboard side, down low near the bow. The most vulnerable spot for torpedoes they say. Which is fine with me.

VII

It felt strange being on the sea after living so long by its edge. The headlands he was used to, the beaches, the coves. It was as if they were flimsy props that had fallen away, revealing the overwhelming vastness of the stage. He felt an unaccountable shyness before it, as if he wasn't quite man enough to face the vastness alone. It was a jurisdiction he had no sway over. On the island, at the sea's edge, he felt he was living within a realm that posed simple, direct questions, and here was a totally separate realm where there was only one question, a big one you had to bob up and down on without expecting an answer.

A beautifully asked question—that was something he wouldn't have expected, not in the North Atlantic, not in winter. The sun jumped through the gray horizon and blasted it to gold, forcing the water into the same color, at least for the dawn's first few minutes. Later, the sea chilled itself into a vivid green color, but wait long enough and the sun would get behind the ship and descend again, bringing back the gold, only burnished this time, softer. The wind came from the west—gently, more a nudge than a driving force. On all sides the water was riffled with V-shaped combers that seemed in no hurry whatsoever, along for the ride, a convoy of cream-colored foam. It was a wonderful sight, a won-

32

derful sea, a wonderful crossing. A man standing near the rail could get lost merely staring down at it. A man could easily get lost.

On that first night he did not go to dinner. He slept well enough, though he woke up once, startled by an agonized whining sound that seemed to emerge from the initial-scratched plating at the head of his bunk. It was obviously some trick between the wind and the metal—the sea talking, nothing more. In the morning, dressed warmly, he began a slow circuit of the deck, trying to get a sense of the ship and its passengers while the good weather lured most of them outside.

They were a varied mix. American officers on their way overseas and not looking very happy about it—paunchy men, wearing their Sam Browne belts in a way that suggested hernias and trusses. A few Canadian officers who, judging by their expressions, their solemn way of staring out over the ocean, had seen their share of fighting. Businessmen looking like businessmen everywhere, no richer, no sleeker, so it was hard to imagine them being profiteers. Two Japanese diplomats, always together, always smiling, very conscious of the need to keep up appearances. An elderly couple who spoke with heavy German accents which would have gotten them into trouble if they weren't so obviously harmless.

Promenading in ones and twos around the deck, taking up all the public room on the ship, was an entirely different category, one that, as the tout back on the pier had promised, was composed entirely of women. There were dozens of them—no, hundreds. A few were in their fifties or sixties, mothers who, having lost a son, had found the strength and the money to make the passage to fetch back their remains. Most, the overwhelming majority, were much younger, women who had lost their husbands. A few of these, women from Quebec or the prairies, wore black and looked mournful. The majority, the Americans, wore chic traveling clothes and looked numb.

Their days were filled with this solemn clockwise promenading, like skaters in a very grave waltz, enlivened only by clumsy boat drills that left everyone confused. Every swirl that differed in pattern from the riffles that accompanied the ship's wake, every new glint of sunlight, and someone was bound to point and gasp, convinced it was a torpedo. Once, as Marden stood by the rail squinting with everyone else, an American major shoved a knowing elbow in his side.

"U-boats!" he scoffed. "Ice is the real danger. We're steaming far too north for my liking. She wouldn't be the first Cunarder to come a cropper on a berg."

They had an alarm that night, just after dark. A siren went off—there was a heavy chirping sound as the ship's one gun opened up from the bow. It was a comic sound, not a threatening one, and it was matched by the echo of doors slamming open as passengers rushed out into the corridor demanding of the stewards an explanation.

The false alarm had one effect—it made Marden decide to dress and go to dinner. The maitre d', meeting him at the top of the dining room staircase, seemed grateful for another male. "Mr. Marden?" he said. "If you follow me, I'll show you to your table."

Sitting there was an American colonel, the elderly German couple, eight women traveling alone. One of these, the oldest, most florid, had on a Red Cross uniform, and looked like a rich society woman playing at ambulance driver. But even she wasn't the worst. The worst was an energetic, overdressed woman sitting next to the colonel who looked like the kind of person who, in any social situation whatsoever, would start things off by asking everyone to introduce themselves.

"I know," she said, when Marden pulled his chair out and sat down. "Let's go around the table one by one and tell everyone our name."

Even with the table being mostly American, the introductions didn't get very far. Three people announced their names, but the next person in the circle mumbled something, her neighbor sipped assiduously at her water glass, and that was the end of that. Everyone ate quietly, at least at first. All of the women had dressed for dinner, and the table was set with as much care and glitter as in peacetime, with roses fresh enough as a centerpiece to complement the women's perfume. But there was no party atmosphere, quite the reverse. The silence was the heavy kind that comes when there is an obvious topic of conversation no one has the energy to address.

Finally, when the first dishes were pulled away but before the entrée, one of the older women took the plunge. "I wonder if I can ask you something, Colonel?" she said, leaning over the table in the old man's direction. "What are conditions like at the front right now? Is it possible for a determined person to reach Brieulles?"

It was obvious the colonel had never heard of such a place. Still, he seemed a kindhearted man, sensitive enough to understand the woman's meaning.

"Brieulles?" he said, stroking his beard. "Near the Argonne forest?"

The woman nodded vigorously up and down—the colonel's lucky guess filled her with hope. "The Bois de Fays they call it. The Wood of the Fairies. Are they fighting there or has the front moved on?"

A pinch-faced woman sitting next to her gently patted her hand; her voice was knowledgeable and dismissive at the same time.

"There is *no* possibility of reaching the front in that sector, my dear. I had a wire from General Ketchum of the Twenty-sixth Division, an old family friend. A person's life would be worth nothing there, even if they could somehow commandeer an automobile for transportation."

The subject broached, everyone seemed anxious to talk at once. The women leaned forward so eagerly their dresses formed a continuous black crease around the table's edge, making it seem they were gathered there for a séance.

Much of the talk was about burials. Was it true that remains were being released to relatives? Some thought it was true, others thought it wasn't. One woman sounded positive on the matter. According to her, formal cemeteries had now been established in eleven of the sectors, but no bodies actually moved yet, and it was these officially identified but still untransferred bodies that a wife could get permission to bring home. Was the Reynal sector free of fighting yet? another woman asked. The Forest de Fere? The Vestle River where the Seventy-seventh Division held the line? What were road conditions like, was it possible to get there by train, hire an automobile, obtain guides? Civilians weren't being allowed to the front in France, but they were allowed very near in Belgium, within twenty kilometers, and wouldn't it be possible to start in Belgium and work your way south? What did the colonel think? Did anyone have any information? Had anyone heard? The Toulon sector? The area around Baccarat?

One woman made the mistake of saying her husband wasn't dead, but in hospital, wounded; she asked the colonel if she needed a special pass to reach his side. The other women stared at her as if she were guilty of saying something unbearably cruel. How much they would give to have a husband who was merely wounded!

The talk was fast, passionate—again came the feeling they were trying to levitate the table by sheer wishing. Only one other person besides Marden took no part in this—one of the younger women, sitting directly opposite him. She had been one of those who announced her name, Susan Marshall, and he surprised himself by remembering it. She was dressed more simply than the other women; the black seemed more foreign to her, and clashed with her girlish complexion. She pressed forward as rigidly, as hopefully, as the others, but there was something in her that wouldn't let her speak. She caught his eye once. Their joint silence, as if usual in such cases, became a bond that separated them from the others.

The overdressed woman was talking now, the one who tried to get the introductions started. She had an accent that Marden thought might be of Boston, affected, mincing, and yet what she said was sincere enough, bewildered enough, to stand as the summary of all they felt.

"What does missing mean, actually *mean*? Is it missing like an ashtray goes missing, something that might turn up at any moment? Or is it missing like missing someone you love who's temporarily away in the country? Missing? Why don't they spell it out? Your husband is missing which means he's killed only we don't know where his body is so that's what we're going to call it. Or your husband is missing and that probably means the Germans have him and his name will appear on a Red Cross ledger in due course. What exact percentage of missing end up found? Men get lost, turn up in different units. I know a woman in Quincy whose son did just that and he's home with her today. France is a maze, think of the confusion. Cannon go missing, tanks go missing, whole trenches disappear. Or think of a bullet. It can miss, can't it? It can go missing overhead so it harms no one. I think of the word constantly, ever since the telegram came. I feel it like a hand around my throat sometimes, and other times I feel like it's a needle in my eye and I can't get my mind around it. *Missing*. What on earth can that mean?"

No one at the table could help her. They looked at each other, sought comfort in their mutual confusion, put a decent amount of silence around the question, but then dessert came, and the chatter, the questions, the desperation, started once again.

☙

Tired of it, so came back here to write down a few words, but not before a detour. Ship's library. The second officer, a decent man, told me about it yesterday, and I thought I might go there and find an atlas. A cramped, musty old place used mostly for storage. Wine bottles, folded deck chairs, a few dusty books. Found my atlas, was looking through it trying to locate a map of Belgium, when the door opened and into the room walked the quiet woman from dinner, Susan Marshall, come to search the maps, too.

We talked, surprisingly easily. She has her story ready, has obviously told it many times. Her husband a captain in the Fourth Division, killed on patrol near St. Mihiel, a man who hated soldiering, but had rigid ideas about patriotism and honor. I had very little to give back to her. No story yet, nothing I can do but mumble. A spirited woman, looks right up at you with that American forthrightness, the energy nothing can stop, though from what I've seen here, they become more like Canadians with death. Tones them down. Blue eyes much brighter than what she realizes probably. They exist independently of her mood. Age thirty-five, thirty-six. "I'm trying to find where a village called Hatton-chatel is," she said. Belgium map was a bad one, showing only Brussels and Dunkirk, but the French one was better, and by holding it up to the light we managed to find her village. Traced with her finger a line up to where Ypres should be. How many boys lie under that line? Noticed she was cold, shivering, but had no coat to give her. We talked some more, little things, the voyage. Her husband once wrote her a letter and said the Canadian troops were the finest on the Western Front. In an odd way I envied her, her spirit. The way I envied the man who leapt off the train.

He hesitated now, actually put the pencil down beside his diary to listen. It was plain enough. There in the steel, running down the side, taking residence in the plating. He tried isolating it from the deep throb of the turbines that was there all the time.

The whining sound again, he wrote. Not whining, but something deeper, throatier, more essential. I would say from a storm, but the sea is calm, no rolling. Only present at night. Owls, terrified, might make such a sound. Unfathomable distress. What mechanism accounts for it? Grit in the turbines? The complaints of gears? Must remember to ask the second officer for an explanation.

VIII

Susan Marshall spent much of the next day with him, the third at sea. The weather continued fine, so much of this was on deck, leaning up against the rail, or sitting in deck chairs, her with a blanket around her shoulders, him braving it out with only his coat. She could talk easily and calmly about her husband. He had been a lawyer in small-town Ohio, a man who served on the boards of charities, volunteered his time—the kind of good, stolid, accepting man who wouldn't give history any problems. Marden, for his part, didn't mention Laura's name at all. He could only face what lay ahead of him; there was no room in the channel, the current toward the east ran too strong, to turn and confront what he had left behind. Even about Billy he said very little. He explained how he had been offered a commission from the ranks, time to train, a respite from the trenches—how he had turned this down, Billy being more rebellious than Susan's husband, more questioning. And yet history hadn't had any trouble disposing of him either.

She didn't like it when he talked that way—his gentle attempts at cynicism were always met with her disapproving frown. But she looked splendid, frowning. The tsk-tsk earnestness behind it, the way her little body seemed too small to back it up, and yet tried backing it up anyway. He treated himself to that, just the way he treated himself to the sunlight, the warmth that came when it touched their faces.

When it was time for lunch they stayed where they were, so for an hour they walked the deck alone. Not at first, but quickly, they began holding themselves the way two people do who have long been together, accommodating themselves to each other's posture, straying a certain distance but never beyond that before coming back to the space that was now mutually theirs.

"There's a ship," she said, for the third or fourth time. She was childishly proud of her eyes.

"A neutral probably. If there are any neutrals left."

She shielded her forehead with her hand, as if squinting to see the ship's name. "Peru. There's always Peru."

He nodded. "Ah, Peru."

The word itself seemed calming, the one point in the world the war didn't cover. But it would. The war would last long enough to drown even Peru. He stared toward the lonely blaze of sunlight she thought was a ship, tried bringing his pity to it, the horizontal smudge that met the horizon and steamed heedlessly on.

"Two days left now," she said, looking up at him. "To Southampton I mean. I wonder what we'll find there."

"In England? Very simple. Base headquarters for my son's regiment. News of him there. Details. The exact coordinates of where he died."

"And after that?"

"To Flanders. If I can get there. And you to France."

"They *are* letting civilians up to the line. I don't care what those horrid women say. Not the very trenches, but as close as a mile back. The front has moved on. I've written letters, made inquiries. There's no question but that it's moved eastward."

"Yes. Until the Germans attack again, and then people like you and me may see more than we want."

"In Richard's last letter home he described a forest they were near. All the forests in France have names, but not this one, it was too small. It was surrounded by a swamp, so no one could build a trench there, it acted like a moat. The shells had missed it, the poison gas. So there were still beech trees, leaves, even birds. He used to stare at it all day through his periscope, he wrote. It brought him peace. That's what I want to find. The woods that brought him peace."

There was so much determination in her, so much energy, he was certain she would find it. Peace. Yes. A personal kind of peace. Peace for Susan Marshall. And yet these kinds of words made him feel uncomfortable—it wasn't far removed from talking of angels and fairies.

"I saw a man killed by blast once," he said, speaking

very softly. "It was a logging train, a small-gauge loco-motive with a boiler that jammed. It wasn't particularly horrible, the sight of him. What was horrible was how fate snapped its fingers and in an instant this man was nothing. Nothing. Here a moment before the explosion I didn't even know Nothing was a force in the world, let alone the most powerful force. It taught me a lesson I was wrong to forget."

Her lips tightened—around the rail, her delicate hands turned white—and yet he could see her trying to fight through it and understand.

"You expect nothing? Then why go?"

"To expect nothing. I want to see the exact spot my son was killed to teach myself to expect nothing. If I don't, if I had stayed in Canada, I would go through what remains of my life with expectation. Every time a letter comes or a step sounds on the path or a boat stands in toward shore, I'll say to myself, 'Ah yes, it's Billy come home at last.' To have expectation after this"—he spread his arms apart—"is intolerable. That's the one lesson to come out of this war. Man needs to bury the expectant part where it won't bother us again."

"Yes," she said, frowning, not bothering to hide her distress. "But you expect something now. Everyone here does. The telegrams, the official notification. None of that matters. We expect to find them, no matter what we say. Deep in our hearts we expect to find them wait-ing for us when we reach France."

"There was one part of the engine driver that was found. A button. He was a great ladies' man, a back-woods Casanova. The only part of him they found was a button off his fly."

She turned toward him—yes, argue more, he said, or tried making his eyes say; talk me out of it, tell me I'm wrong—but he had gone too far this time, and without saying anything, turning as abruptly as if he had slapped her, she crossed to the iron doorway and disappeared.

She didn't come to dinner that night. A woman transferred over from one of the other tables, so there wasn't even a gap where her place had been. Unlike the previous night, conversations were desultory—no one had the strength to lift the blanket of silence that had collapsed over their heads. Only the elderly couple, the tourists with the German accents, seemed at all animated. They went from table to table taking pictures with their Brownie camera, forcing everyone to smile.

Marden stood it as long as he could, then excused himself and walked out to the main promenade. Restless, filled with an energy he knew could turn on him at any second, he walked as fast and determinedly as the confines of the ship allowed. He couldn't face going back to his cabin, he knew that much. After five laps, six laps, seven, he broke off and headed for the library, groped in the darkness until he found the light switch, started poring once more through the atlas and its maddeningly obscure maps.

His nerves did turn and very quickly. He grew furious with the map, the way it hid more than it revealed. Bloody Amsterdam, a Brussels he could care less about, a worthless Antwerp. Where were the places that mattered, the killing places, the places boys died? He tore out the page by its edge, then the next one, then the one after that, crumpling them up into balls, throwing them furiously toward the floor. Belgium, France, England,

Germany. He had ripped the whole atlas apart, he was standing there staring dumbly down at the fat crinkled balls made by the paper, when the door opened, and Susan Marshall entered as she had the night before, silently, smoothly, as if bearing in her slender form the gift of grace itself.

She saw him standing there, saw the litter on the floor, appraised, with those quick eyes of hers, exactly how things stood. She stooped as if to neaten things, then immediately stood up again and continued across the carpet toward him. Her arm came up, found his, pressed something warm and sharp into his hand.

"Poor man!" she whispered.

She was back out the door before he realized what it was—a key, a brass room key with a number engraved on the side. Only slowly did the warmth from her hand leave the metal. He clasped it in his palm, clasped it hard, but stood where he was for a long few minutes, his head tilted down in the posture of someone smoking a pipe. He needed those minutes to measure as precisely as he could the extent of his need, to remember this later, not judge wrong.

Her cabin was on the upper deck, which meant he had to walk outside to the companionway, giving him just enough time to see the brilliant dust of the stars, take their coolness on his face. Coming back in, he made a wrong turn. For a moment he hesitated, unsure exactly where in the ship he stood. The lights were always lowered at night for protection from U-boats. As on previous nights, everyone retired early, including the stewards, so the hallway was deserted.

He decided to go right, had actually started in that

direction, when a sound in the wall made him stop where he was. A humming noise, but much shriller, giving it a mechanical quality, like a spindle spinning too fast, or a lathe cutting too deep. He was slow in connecting it to the sound he had heard the previous night and the night before that, the whining that emerged from the ship's plating. Slow—but then quickly certain. It was the same sound, only closer here to its source.

The nearest cabin had a little plaque, 15B. He moved against the door. This time it was plain enough. Crying. Inside the cabin someone was crying. A woman crying. It wasn't normal crying, sad crying, but something a hundred times more essential and desperate, as if the sadness, as it emerged from the woman's throat, was being tortured and flailed.

He pushed on the door, but it was locked. He decided to go for the steward, had started up the corridor, when he heard another sound coming from the next cabin down, 17B. It was the same kind of sound, only from a weaker source. Softer wails, coming quicker, with gagging intakes of breath.

He put his mouth to the door. "Hello?" he said dumbly. "Do you require any help?"

Stupid of him. Insane. Across the hallway another woman cried, this one in coughs and hiccoughs that made him think of a little girl whose crying had gone on so long it had taken on a life independent of the throat it came from. He pushed against her door, knowing it would be locked, but feeling the need to place his hand on the sound, quiet it, make it go still. Further down the corridor, where it turned left and headed for the boat deck stairs, the sound was louder. It was as if all the individual crying had joined forces in the center of the corridor; the crying was now in chorus. Move close to one side and he could differentiate the individual wails, but there in the middle all he was conscious of was the mutuality of it, the way the sound seemed precisely balanced, one half drilling him in one ear, the other half boring in on the other.

He walked quickly outside, groped in the darkness until he found the companionway, tried the next deck up. At first this was better, all was silent and calm; on the carpet were traces of cigar ash, so it was obvious these cabins held the businessmen and the colonels. He could smell spilled whisky with the ash—it was a noxious smell, reeking of smugness and complacency, and he hurried away from it as he had the crying.

Toward the end of the corridor the sound came back again. He heard a woman keening, keening in the old sense of the word, so he could picture her rocking back and forth on her bed, tearing wildly at the matted hair across her face. Another woman moaned as women do in love, only the sound mocked itself as it emerged, became far too tremulous and empty. Another woman cried as if she were cursing out her sadness, spitting it defiantly toward heaven—here, for the first time, he heard fists beating against the wall. Another woman, many women, repeatedly shouted out their sons', their husbands' names. *Stephen!* they shouted. *Donald! Michael! Jim!* In the last cabin on that deck a woman screamed over and over again, seemingly intent on making her despair the loudest in the ship. Pierced by it, the lights in the passageway sizzled, blinked brilliantly, went out. Beneath him he could feel the ship change course, begin its zigzag evasions; he heard far above him the sound of the siren, as if all the sounds bottled up inside the ship had emerged there at last in one synchronized, animal-like cry.

He stumbled forward with his hands out to keep from hitting anything, only now the sound seemed palpable, a pressing force, and flail as desperately as he could, there was no brushing past. He covered his ears, but that didn't help either. The crying jumped down his throat, injected itself into his veins, sank cold and deadening toward his groin. He tried one corridor after the other, but no matter which way he stumbled the crying was always there waiting for him, until he was on the point of screaming himself just to press back with something commensurate. He was lost, wanting nothing now but to get away from it, smother the sound, beat it from his ears, stumble back to his cabin, fall against his bunk and let the sound flatten him, flatten him utterly, past all hope, all expectancy, all caring.

He made it there, in the end. Hands shaking, he lit his pipe. He sat there quietly. He tried bluffing his nerves back to normal, breathing in long slow breaths that never seemed to find his lungs. In time, the siren stopped. The ship quieted. The wailing re-established itself in the plating, took on a steely sound, thinning so gradually that by the first gray streaks of morning it was hardly a sound at all.

❧

During the last two days of the crossing nothing forced itself into his diary, nothing he had strength for, or just one incident alone.

Nov. 9. Picked up pilot off Southampton at 8:36. Ships on the horizon, tugs, submarine nets and buoys, making it seem like Halifax harbor has been towed here ahead of us and lies waiting exactly as it was when we left. The German couple are said to be sick, one in a bad way. Spanish flu. A collection taken up to bribe the steward not to report it for two hours, thereby avoiding quarantine until the rest of us are off the ship. I gave my share, called the steward back, gave double.

IX

"Ticket to Salisbury? Ah yes, a lovely striped one, let me reach back and—There, sir. All stamped and proper. Canadian, do you mind my asking? Thought so. A Yank would push right up to the head of the queue, knock aside the ladies. First time over? England's green and pleasant land we call it. That would be Blake, sir. English mystic? Then we have our local lad, Squire Hardy, who you could pop in on if you left the train at Dorchester. Kipling's been awfully silent these days—nothing cheery to say. His son Jack fallen at Loos . . . Listen to us! A regular literary conversation! We don't get many going toward Salisbury these days, only the odd military gent. London's more the ticket for first-timers like yourself. Of course Salisbury has its cathedral. Thirteenth century and very fine. Then there are the Great Stones, megalithic monument, very fine also. Easy to picture those who built it, sweating and slaving, some great hulk of a Druid beating them on with his whip. Lots of sights around Salisbury, sir, but you'll be wanting to

49

press on to London as fast as possible. Finest city in the world. There's the Abbey and St. Paul's and St. Bartholomew the Great and St. Clement Danes and St. Giles Cripplegate and the Guildhall and Lincoln's Inn and Buckingham Palace and Madam Tussauds and Hyde Park and the Zoological Gardens and the docks which are worth a visit, don't let anyone tell you differently, particularly down by Wapping. And even those are nothing compared to the greatest attraction, the Tower of London, place where Mary Stuart lost her head. A chap could spend an entire morning there and not be bored, and there's going to be more soon, more worth seeing, because one fine day this war will end, and when it does on display in the Tower will be the Kaiser's bloody testicle, or at least the one sorry shriveled glob that's all he has."

X

The ticket clerk was right—Marden did feel like a tourist, especially that first afternoon. He had gone through life with a certain picture in his mind of England, what it looked like, and here the picture was streaming past the train's window, correct to the smallest detail. Thatched cottages? There they were past the telegraph poles, with wire mesh so the birds couldn't pluck apart the straw. Tudor mansions with crisscrossed beams? There they were on the ridge lines, framed by copses of willow and beech, sheep grazing in the surrounding meadows. Pubs? He could see their signs. Quaintness? It was everywhere. Greenness? It all but smothered him in richness, brightened by a sun that belonged more to May than it did November.

There wasn't the slightest hint it was a country at war. He knew a surgeon in Vancouver who had returned from serving at the front. The flesh leading down to a sniper wound was apt to be unusually soft, the surgeon told him—not red, but a gentle rose color, without a blemish of any kind, not until you came to the actual entry spot, where, of course, it was all quite different. It was this kind of flesh he was looking at now, the rosy skin smoothed by the tug of a bullet hole he hadn't yet found.

The train climbed slightly, enough to put a tilt in the car—now came the famous Salisbury Plain. Out the window, crucified to a tree, was a scarecrow left from Guy Fawkes Day, then a winding stream that looked as though it might hold trout, then a village cricket pitch used as an assembly point for the apple harvest, with crates of apples much redder than anything he ever managed back home. A team of laborers piled these onto pallets and then onto a wagon; they were old men, much shabbier, more stooped, than a similar gang of Canadians would be. He would have liked to get out and talk to them, hold an apple in his hand, but already the train was gathering momentum, and the cricket pitch shrank back into insignificance out the window's corner.

The train stopped at all the villages, every crossing. Marden welcomed the slowness. He felt dull, stupid, badly in need of time to think. What puzzled him was this. What he saw out the window, the pastoral land-scape, had some direct connection to the abstraction known as "England," and the abstraction known as "England" had a direct connection to his son's death. What that connection consisted of, the direct causal links, he couldn't understand, or wouldn't understand; he wanted to avoid playing the old tired game, thinking in terms of treaties and entanglements and questions of ancient rights and wrongs. The world's leaders had fallen out among themselves, and this meant bad luck for Billy, and bad luck for millions like him, not only in Canada, but in Scotland and France and Russia and Italy and Serbia and half the countries on the globe. This was as simple and direct an explanation as he was willing to let himself have—and yet his mind raced on.

Arrived Salisbury 5:10 P.M. Found decent enough hotel on the High Street not far from station, the Clovelly. Commercial travelers this morning at breakfast, smoking, laughing loudly over smutty jokes. Walked to the cathedral alongside the Avon, feeling I should make the effort. A funeral in progress. Four funerals, the coffins draped in Union Jacks, the mourners all in black. I went no further. The landlady was helpful in putting me on the right track—a tram out to Cantwell Farm on the edge of the Canadian camp. A long walk still ahead of me, but a farmer came along with a cart full of milk cans going in the same direction. "Off to regiment?" he asked. I nodded and climbed aboard.

A talkative man, though it took me a while to penetrate his accent. Grizzled beard, strong hands, a son fighting in Mesopotamia. Speaks very highly of Canadians, since unlike British they pay cash. The landscape boxed in with hedgerows, cut and channeled by curving lanes—the camp sits above them on the windswept crest of the downs. The sentry waved us through the gate, reached to pat the horse's ear. A formal row of trees giving way to a row of cannon, barrels pointed toward the ground like the necks of shy, burrowing creatures. New cannon—the smell of their oil carried on the breeze. Clumsy-looking American-style tractors past these, row after row, only I had that wrong, because the farmer pointed, shook his head in admiration.

"Tanks. M-fours."

No men around, no soldiers. Tents with rips in their fabric, shredding apart in the wind. All these lorries, cannon, tanks, and not a single soldier visible even on the parade ground, the weapons ready to fight alone now, machine versus machine.

The farmer delivered his milk at the mess hall, pointed me to a Nissen hut a short way beyond underneath a flapping Canadian flag. "Regimental HQ," he said, proud at knowing the lingo. The hut was neat and warm, though bare of any decoration save the king's portrait. In a little anteroom sat a sergeant with a walrus mustache and a lively expression. Had my telegram from Southampton, knew to expect me, who I was.

A stiff manila folder in front of him on the desk.

"Your son's file," he said, when he saw me staring. *File.* Another new wartime word. Made me think of something sharp and raspy, not this stiff, sickly-colored folder centered between his hands. He led me into the next office, put the "file" down on a bigger, shinier desk, saluted the major sitting there, disappeared.

Marden could tell at once the major was a different proposition than the sergeant. He was a wire-thin man, nickel-colored, with the barest dollop of a mustache on a face that was far too pale. His eyes, the corners of his eyes, seemed unnaturally rigid, as if he were forcing back a tic. Too much fighting? Too much boredom? It was hard to tell.

He swiveled back from the window now, looked briefly at the file, but made no move to open it. His appearance suggested a crisp upper-class accent, not the Toronto flatness that came out.

"Look here, Mr. Marden. We've gotten a lot of inquiries like yours. Relatives who have lost a loved one, want to see the place they are interred. True, you are the first father who has actually come to England with his inquiries. Full marks for that. But I will tell you what I write everyone else. There is no visiting the occurrence site until the war is over."

It was no more than Marden expected—the official line. He wondered if the major were man enough to go beyond that.

"It's my understanding the fighting has moved east from Flanders," he said, trying to find a reasonable pitch the major could, by suggestion, follow.

"This is not the information I have."

"I've read newspaper accounts."

"News accounts? Then you will have heard of something called a counter-attack. The Germans are good at it. Damn near ran us back to Amiens last April—you will have read accounts of that, manicured accounts, in those precious newspapers of yours. The Alexandras did not retreat. We stick no matter what happens. Regiments on both flanks up and legged it. Scots, of course—bloody cowards. Left us hanging, but we stuck it anyway."

Marden pointed down to the file. "The letter I received says my son was listed 'killed-missing.' That makes no sense to me, what it means."

"In what way?"

"Was he killed or is he missing?"

"He could easily be both."

"Both?"

"Killed, then missing."

"If he's missing, how can you be sure he was killed?"

"A stretcher team sent to fetch his corpse. Shell finds them. The stretcher bearers all killed, maybe all four, maybe just three. The body blown off the stretcher and sunk in the mud. Red identity disc already gathered, green identity disc left in place on the body. An entry has to be made in company records. Killed-missing. What it means in practical terms is that there is no specific cemetery I can send you to even if I could send you."

Marden listened to this with difficulty. "Can you tell me then," he said, keeping his voice low, "how I could go about visiting the site?" He put his hand up. "Yes, I understand what you're about to say. That there is no telling the exact spot. But surely I can visit the vicinity, see what it was like there."

"What it was like?" The major glared. "You'll need a permit from division headquarters in Ypres, even assuming the front has moved on. To get to Belgium means going to the Dominions office in London and obtaining a travel voucher. They will not give you one, rest assured of that. A sightseeing civilian is the last thing anyone needs at the front. You would require passes all the way along your route, from division down to company level, and if anywhere a man didn't like the look of you, he could turn you back. I tell you this to save a lot of futile effort for all concerned."

It was Marden's cue to get up and leave, but he remained where he was. "The village my son was killed near is called Gheluvelt."

It was the first time he had said the word out loud—it felt soft and harmless in his mouth, not hard and spiky the way it lay in his imagination. Strange—but not as strange as the major's reaction. If he looked bitter and dismissive before, it was nothing compared to the expression that came across his face now. His eyes blinked this time, the corners squeezing tight; his little mustache shrank toward his nose.

"You must be mistaken. The regiment fought near no village called Gheluvelt."

"I had a letter from your Colonel Vickers, my son's commanding officer."

"There is a mistake. Your information is wrong. People become confused in time of war. There is no mention in the regiment's records of any village by that name."

His tone was as hard and impassive as his face. Marden knew from long experience there was no softening a man off that once it took hold. He stood up before the major did, walked ahead of him toward the door.

"You will have to come back when the war ends," the major said—it was like being hit in the back by an icicle. "When it ends. In thirty years."

The sergeant wasn't in place behind the desk. Marden found him outside near the steps, with his head craned back against the siding, staring up at the slate-colored sky.

"Smoke?" he asked, holding out a pack of Woodbines.

Marden knew what the gesture meant, so he took one, let the sergeant light it, stood beside him staring out the same direction as if their words could meet neutrally there, off the record.

"Was the major helpful then?" the sergeant asked.

"That depends," Marden said carefully. "Was he in France?"

The sergeant nodded. "Three years. Mentioned in dispatches, the Military Cross."

"And?"

"A bit of shellshock. Not much. Not enough to get him sent home."

Off in the distance past the mess hall came a heavy clanking sound it was impossible for Marden to identify. It was as if the assembled tanks and cannon, bored with waiting, were bumping shoulders in agitation, swiveling their turrets, spinning angrily their gears.

"Corporal William Marden, is that right?"

"Yes."

"Heard of him, never met. Good runner. Battalion sports—the long-distance events. It was my job to get the trophy inscribed with the winners, so I recall the name. And you're not the only one who's come asking about him either. The day before yesterday there was someone else."

The words, simple as they were, hammered Marden on the heart. "Someone else?"

"Little slip of a girl. Wool coat bigger than she was. Couldn't have been more than eighteen. Elaine Reed's the name. Here, I wrote it down."

He handed over a square of paper with some words neatly inked across the side. "She asked about where he's buried. What cemetery it is. Of course I couldn't tell her very much beyond the little she already knew."

The surprise hadn't had time to settle yet—Marden brought out the first inane question that came to mind. "What did she know?"

"Well, I've thought of that. Not what, but how. Not his wife if you take my point. Army would have no record of her existence. Sweethearts? As far as the army is concerned, there is no such category. My theory is this. There must have been a mate of his who knew about her, wrote her the news. Mates will promise each other that, before a push. That's the only explanation that makes sense."

The sergeant pointed again to the paper. "There are two addresses she left, if I found any information for her. The one, as you can see, is her home there in Sage. The second is a hotel in London, the Adelaide on High Holborn. She said if I couldn't contact her at one I could contact her at the other. A little slip of a girl really, except for that coat. It's odd, but I got the impression she had never been away from home before, not even this far. Way she held herself. All careful and fragile if you take my point."

Marden glanced down at the paper. "Sage?"

"Not far, sir. Walking distance for a soldier. A good Sunday stroll. You follow the road down from camp, and there's a track across the downs that saves some distance. I would think she would be a good person to talk to, if you can get past her shyness." He stubbed the cigarette out on the siding, threw the butt toward his boot. "Good luck, sir. Safe journey."

Marden sensed the sergeant hadn't told him everything—and yet, from sheer goodness, he had told him a great deal. Immediately, he remembered the last letter Billy had sent home, the mention of a girl he had gone walking with. Was it this Elaine girl, Elaine Reed? The sergeant stood there waving and pointing to get him started in the right direction; leaving the camp, he turned and raised his arm, then started along the road that wound slowly down the windswept path.

XI

It felt good to be walking again, have his fate depend on his own muscles. He was badly out of shape, but the grade was easy and he made good time. Just when he decided he had missed the track, he came to a crude wooden sign. *Sage,* it read, with an arrow pointing toward a path.

This was the way Billy and his friends must have come on their Sunday outings; for the first time he was doing what he had set out to do, walk in his son's footsteps. Literally so. The dirt was damp enough that bootprints were clearly discernible, the hobnail patterns, and there on the higher side of the path they had petrified under the sun. It was easy to imagine what it must have felt like. The youthful high spirits, the overwhelming sense of release, the summer sun and how it baked the soreness out after a solid week of drill. Too easy in its way—Marden wasn't ready for the suddenness. The longer he walked, the more he found himself trying to force all such impressions away. Better to concentrate on what he could see around him, the simple facts of the day. Talk to the girl, see what she amounted to, and then he could start putting their story together, but not until then.

The landscape was lusher than anything he had seen so far. Pasturage, most of it—hay fields that hadn't been cut, so the tassels came up past his waist. In the distance, stick figures tended fires of stump and brush, pruning out the hedgerows; pillars of blue-gray smoke rose in every direction, furled ones, wrapped tightly by the heavy air. In the sheltered places flowers still bloomed— dainty English flowers he didn't have a name for. Robins called in a way no Canadian birds could manage, even in springtime; rooks soared on the updrafts, in no hurry to descend. Everywhere lay peace and contentment and stillness, the kind of quiet that only comes when it's lasted centuries—and yet, much as he longed to let himself give way to it, something resisted, fought back. No, he wouldn't let England seduce him so easily, fool him, play him for a sucker.

Sage was the natural culmination of all this beauty. It

lay hidden by a low hill until he was in its midst—a dozen houses of yellow-gray stone, a stream along the edge of them, a cobblestoned High Street and several narrow lanes winding up the hill. Everything seemed exactly where it should be. The stone church, the vicarage, the post office, the blacksmith's—a row of shops leading to a town hall that doubled as the doctor's surgery. There was a tea room, a watering trough for horses, a green with benches where farmers coming in from the country could sit and talk. If civilization consisted of the simplest, most essential expression of a landscape and its people, then Sage, Marden decided, was the most civilized place he had ever been.

It wasn't hard finding where the girl lived. The third house past the church had a vine-draped fence with a copper plaque: *Hawthorn Cottage A. Reed.* It was a slightly larger house than the others, built of stone and stucco, centuries old. A small terrace had been added to the front, a wall not quite hiding a compact garden that had been carefully spaded over for winter.

Marden walked around behind the house toward the solid, rhythmic sound of chopping. A man in a tweed vest stood splitting kindling on what looked to be an old forge. He was younger than Marden, in his forties at most—an intelligent-looking, dark-complexioned man, who, Marden guessed, was probably master of the village school.

"Yes?" he said, looking up now.

There was no subtle way for him. "My name is Charles Marden. I have reason to believe your daughter knew my son."

The man's eyes—it was as if there were a wire pulling

them—jerked to the side. Marden followed them, saw the one detail in the village he hadn't noticed before, a small train station visible behind the slant of the town hall's roof. It wasn't hard to make the connection. Reed had been expecting someone, though not him.

He brought his eyes back with difficulty, laid the hatchet on the forge, nodded slowly up and down. "You had better come in."

The house was smaller than it looked from the road. Wooden ship models were scattered about in various stages of completion, there were hundreds of books, and hanging on the wall were intricate embroideries of scenes that looked to be out of King Arthur. Marden, not for the first time, marveled at what secret fortresses people could build for themselves against the horrors of the world. Though the curtains were drawn, with no lamps burning, the rooms seemed bursting with the energy of light.

Mr. Reed showed him to a seat near the largest bookcase, then disappeared. When he came back, long minutes later, it was with a plump, middle-aged woman with commonplace features that managed somehow to be graceful. Was it grief that brought this out? The lines in her face looked recent, her eyes were red from what might be sleeplessness, and yet, company calling, she could still observe the decencies and pull herself together.

She sat down opposite him on a sofa. Mr. Reed, with obvious reluctance, sat down, too.

"We were very sorry to learn of your son's death," Mrs. Reed said in a quiet voice. "There are so many we feel sorry for. As a father, this won't be much comfort for you, but it's all we have."

Marden nodded his thanks—looked up at them to make sure it got through. Mrs. Reed, though, was not the kind to need any prompting. She understood why he was there, and so wasted no time.

"It was Adel Barston's idea. Of course, it's always Adel's idea, she means so well. A theatrical evening for the whole village to celebrate spring and raise our spirits. Some poetry and a recitation and the children singing. Fran Wable has a wonderful tenor, he was once on the stage, and so he would sing, too. It was a full evening's entertainment, it didn't end until after midnight, and there were marvelous Chinese lanterns for people to walk beneath. But we were talking, arranging things in advance, and it occurred to us it would be a fine thing to invite the Canadian boys down from their hill."

Outside, muffled, came the sound of a train whistle. Both the Reeds exchanged glances, seemed to sit even more stiffly on the edge of the sofa, though Mrs. Reed's voice remained calm.

"Your son came. Elaine met him at the booth she ran selling cider and punch. He visited twice to the house, once in late June, then another time in July, just before his regiment left. Apparently this was enough to form a very deep—bond. A letter from Flanders arrived two weeks ago. I handed it to her. She became—agitated. She didn't cry, she doesn't cry, but in the morning, after she had left to teach her class, I found strands of hair on the pillow, her beautiful hair, which she had torn out from her scalp."

Her words were too simple, too direct—they hung in the air between the sofa and his chair as if they had turned solid. Mr. Reed, with the kind of shuddering a dog makes, got abruptly to his feet.

"I must be going, Mr. Marden. I have a class I must take." He glanced down at his wife. "Peter's class. He's feeling ill."

"Peter? I saw him this morning."

"Feverish. A tightness in his neck. It came on suddenly. Doctor Sutton has been summoned. Goodbye, Mr. Marden. I'm sure my wife will try to answer any questions you might have."

This was said kindly, formally, but there was no disguising the fact he found the situation intolerable. Mrs. Reed walked him to the door—Marden could hear their soft, whispered exchanges—and then she came back again, looking more anxious than before, as if the pretence at normalcy, with her husband gone, required too much effort to maintain.

"Elaine is not here. She has—left. When my husband saw you coming up the walk he thought it might be a telegram. So he was disappointed, it's hard for him to be his usual self. She left suddenly two days ago, on Thursday. She had some money from teaching her class, and that money is gone from her bureau, along with a bag and some clothing."

The simple facts—and yet they weren't enough for her, she hurried on as if trying to fill in the mystery before it got out of hand.

"I have a sister in Belfast, her favorite aunt. I'm sure it's there she's gone, to get over her—bereavement. With the war, the trains are so crowded, she may have only just arrived. The telegraph is slow, the telephone connections. Mr. Reed and I have decided that tomorrow is the earliest date we could possibly hear from her."

"Could she have gone to London?" Marden asked.

"London? What on earth for? No, I'm sure she's gone to her aunt's."

The explanation, said out loud, must not have offered as much comfort as she hoped, because she frowned now, and the lines she had forced away settled back over her face.

"What's so odd is that she's the last girl who would go off that way. She has never done anything like this. Some girls are wild to go to the city, but Elaine has always been a homebody. Church, school, going riding, helping out where she can. She takes the smallest children at school, the bashful ones, because there's so much of that in her. She went to Swindon once to visit a friend, and she got lost on the train, just going that far. We had a good laugh about it, but she was too shy to ask anyone for help. She walked all the way home, twenty miles."

Marden nodded, asked some gentle questions—and yet felt there was much she wasn't telling him, just as he had sensed a hesitation in the otherwise helpful sergeant. But maybe this had something to do with the war. That all explanations seemed partial now, even ones that dealt with a single individual.

"Your William was good for her," Mrs. Reed was saying. "He brought something out in her that was colorful and bright. I only met him the second time he came, which was just before his regiment left. Did you notice the oak tree down our road? Cromwell's Oak they call it, since he had lunch under it once. William was admiring it, he said it was nearly as tall as the trees you have in Canada, and I said something about it being a pity, such nice shade and everyone afraid to sit beneath it because of the rotten limb near the top. He asked if I knew where he could find a saw. I thought of Harold's, and quicker than that he was scrambling up the side of the tree like it was something he did every day of his life. That limb came down fast enough it did. Elaine stood there laughing and clapping him on."

On his way out she showed him a photograph taken early in the summer for Elaine's eighteenth birthday. She had alert and surprisingly forceful features, given her mother's description. Big eyes on an oval face, delicate forehead, long and luxurious hair. The photograph had been hand-tinted, but not very well, making her cheeks so red they looked rouged, and yet, by luck or by skill, it managed to capture something secret in her expression. This, he decided, staring down, is how she must look when no one is watching—and if Billy saw this in her, everything was easier to understand.

Mrs. Reed was doing some appraising of her own. "He favored you," she said, as if this were only plain now that they were outdoors. "The same cheekbones. The eyes. The sandy hair."

"My wife always claimed he had straw on top, burned yellow from the sun."

"There was a gentleness in him, too. I had that from Elaine, the little she would say."

Marden reached to open the gate.

"Mrs. Reed?"

"Yes?"

"In his last letter home he mentioned going walking with a girl, who I'm sure was your daughter. He said the townspeople were so friendly. He mentioned a country lane. Do you know which that might be?"

"Well yes. Yes, I think so. I saw them walking that direction the day of our tree adventure. Sommers Lane they call it, after the farmer who once lived there. It's the most beautiful walk we have, so I'm sure. You pass the church, take the path through the graveyard, and it begins right there and goes uphill."

"Thank you. I hope things go well for all of you."

"She's not been herself. No, I don't mean the grief, not that alone. A new—note in her. There is another—concern."

"Not ill I hope?"

She didn't answer. Her eyes closed, closed tightly, struggled to come back open. "Oh, not that. Never mind. You go and find the lane, and I'll stand here watching to make sure you've not gone wrong."

XII

He had trouble writing that night in his diary. He would start a sentence, get back up again, stare out the window toward the foggy spire of the cathedral, cross to the opposite window, stare out at the chips shops and tobacconists, count the lonely souls walking past, sit down, hesitate, put down his pen. Facts were one thing, even hard facts, but how to find words for what he had felt that afternoon walking up Sommers Lane? Everyone in the world prayed for peace, longed for peace, spoke of nothing else, and there in the middle of a country lane he had found peace, the essence, hidden there for the duration . . . had found it there, not for himself, something that bathed him in tranquility, but something as external and definite as a box, a carton, he could stare at all he wanted and yet never find the secret of unwrapping.

Mrs. Reed had been right about the beauty. The lane curled back on itself as if it were attempting a circle, then started up the hill in a sinuous winding that remained sensitive to the hill's contours all the way to the top. That it even led uphill seemed to be the lane's secret. It wound so gradually he wasn't aware of putting any effort into the climbing, was surprised at how high onto the downs it eventually led him.

There by the base it was all November, with wet, chestnut-colored leaves covering the dirt, but once the grade rose past the shadow of the church it became much brighter, so it was easy picturing how it looked in summer. The oaks still clung to most of their leaves; the pear trees on the meadow side not only had leaves, but green leaves, and the ferns that lined the embankment remained supple and tall.

There was a word that described the way the trees touched overhead, though he had to struggle to remember it. *Bower.* The trees formed a bower under which, in summer, the sunlight would have been dappled, broken apart into cool shafts. The older trees had a raised network of veins or ridges running up and down their trunks, making it seem as if lovers, in previous centuries, had carved their initials in the bark. Marden, stooping to examine them, ran his hand up and down the most prominent, enjoying the sensation the ridges left on his palm, the rough and ready way they delivered their messages, even if he was too obtuse to know what the messages said.

He wondered which side of the lane they had walked on, Billy and Elaine. The dirt was smooth, there were no tracks other than a cart's down the center, and it seemed natural to cross from side to side, following the fringe of woods on one flank, the high meadow on the other. The briars in the meadow were parted back in a rough path; the uncut hay, with the same pliancy, lay flattened in a circle, one that, with winter coming, would not spring back. Marden sensed that if he went there, touched the earth with his hand, it would still be warm.

Had they walked that way then, taken a detour that intersected the road further along? The meadow lay far enough over the village that the steeples and eaves were visible sticking up from the broad halo of coal smoke that had settled with afternoon. It would have been tempting, for anyone strolling in the summer, to sit there enjoying the sunshine, the softness of the meadow grass, the way it formed its own secret bower, the yielding earth, the silence.

The silence. A little way on he came to a flat stone laid across two smaller stones as a bench, likely for the woman of the vanished farm, to rest on her long walk home from market. Marden sat there staring out toward the meadow, trying to feel what the two young people had felt, then suddenly closed his eyes, as if stricken by a pain. It was the quiet he focused on. It was a quiet he had never experienced before—a quiet, he knew instinctively, that must be richer, more total, than any other place's in the world. Take beauty, sweetness, longing, press it into the smallest space, the briefest moment, and this is what you would have. A garden, a paradise garden like this.

He felt dizzy in it, not so much the silence as what the silence let in. For a moment he was sure he was suffering an attack after all, though there were no symptoms he could identify, nothing that spasmed, labored or hurt. Something else was driving deep in him, an intuition, a warning intuition that used the rhythm of his heart to drive home its message. This is as close as you can come, stop here, his heart told him. *Stop here.*

He wasn't sure how long the moment on the bench lasted. A minute? Ten minutes? Just as the quiet took the lane out of the world, it removed it from time, in a way he had never known, so it was no wonder he felt dizzy. In the end it passed, just as any spell passes. He got to his feet, felt himself over like a man knocked down in an accident, then began walking slowly, stiffly, back down the road toward the church. At the bottom of the lane, stooping suddenly, he picked up a pebble, a striated blue one the size of a child's marble—he stooped for it, felt it, and then, the pain sharp and real this time, threw it with all his might away.

Next morning, he woke up early to take the first train to London.

XIII

An exhausting, difficult day to make sense of, topped off now by—*this*. Began ordinarily enough. A real November morning, dark and rainy, so even at seven it was still pitch black. Only a few people boarded the train. Businessmen on their way into the city, reading, frowning over the *Times*. Three pensioners playing cards on each other's knees. The porter unable to convince anyone to buy from his meagerly stocked cart. Daylight finally came, but it was better off being dark, the little difference it made. The industrial suburbs, the train sunk low in them, so it seemed we were tunneling through slag.

Unexpected delays, some as long as twenty minutes—the conductor was puzzled, offered no explanation. Then the odd thing occurs. As we gather speed again, out the window, standing on top of the embankment silhouetted against the gray sky, appears an old man who must be ninety. He is wearing an ancient red uniform with medals and ribbons. But it's not what he's wearing that catches my attention, it's what he is doing. He holds a cane in his right hand—and as he sees us pass, he raises it high over his head, brings it back down, then pumps it high again, stands there doing this over and over, in a grotesque kind of drill.

A hundred yards down the track, passing through a zone of warehouses, someone else appears on the embankment, this time a little boy, wearing what must be his father's mackintosh. He shoves his hand free of the sleeve like a magician, and on the end of it, burning brightly, is a Roman candle, tossing off pink and white sparks. He holds it up so we can see—the entire show is for the train. A bit further on comes a gang of older boys with an entire arsenal of sparklers, which they dare each other with by shoving them in each other's faces, then, seeing us, lob them happily toward the tracks.

I tried remembering what national holiday this was, couldn't—but then things started happening very fast. More warehouses, but in the gaps between them, ribboned in flashes, people are marching down the street, led by a band of women banging pots and pans. A young girl stands on the roof of one of the factories, demure, quiet-looking. When she sees us she pulls her skirt over her waist, pirouettes around, displays her bottom. A short distance on there's a woman who does her one better. A gang of laborers squats around a bonfire, the men dipping their heads like horses in what looks to be buckets, the women dancing like they're on stage, their arms around each other's shoulders, their dark stubby legs kicking high. A toothless woman takes off her sweater and blouse, stands there shaking her white breasts at us as the men around her laugh uproariously and egg her on. The train lurches to a stop. The conductor sticks his head in from the next car, shouts "Pedestrians on the tracks!", disappears. We start up again, the whistle screaming, only now the bonfires are continuous, the dancing people, the sparklers, the flags.

North Kensington—my first real sight of London. Splendid row houses, Regency crescents, dignified squares, only it was difficult to see, it was as if there were wrapping over everything, a living, writhing wrapping, so thick and continuous it was hard at first to understand what the wrapping consisted of. People, people everywhere, clinging to lamp posts, balconies and gables, as if a giant had taken his hand, scooped up thousands, smeared them across the city. At the same time the train was gripped by an enormous pressure, making it seem we had suddenly plunged deep underground. The windows rattled and throbbed in their metal sashes—for a moment I was sure they would break . . . Paddington Station. We stopped at platform nineteen beneath a big clock. The conductors, rather than helping everyone off, rush from the cars first; out the window, racing after them, come the engineers. Even the businessmen, so staid on the journey, are running along the platform, covering their ears and shouting at the same time. Even the pensioners, tossing aside their canes . . . I got off the train last. The huge temple-like station—and high above, like a tolling bell, a chandelier sways back and forth in the wind created by the enormous, the unbelievable, the overwhelming *sound.*

Forced my way up the platform, taken in by the crowd, accepted, shoulders turning, then wedging back, finally carried with them out to the street. The sound is everything—a high guttural hum in which no individual voice survived. Surf is the best analogy, surf during a storm, only there was no ebb to it; just when I thought it could get no louder it grew louder, and this happened every second. It was intensely human. It was as if bones were ground up in it, organs, tissue, and this was the sound that under pressure was wrung out. A bagpipe the size of London, made out of human hearts—that's the best I can do with it. Twelve hours later my ears still ring.

A huge clock in front of the station mounted on a fluted iron column—this becomes the focus of the crowd's attention. The arrow-shaped hands are almost on eleven. Thousands of people hold their arms up making elevens themselves. "Five!" they shout. "Four! . . . Three! . . . Two! . . . ONE!" and then comes a roar that splits, splits quite literally, the sky in half.

❧

The crowd, offered that climax, became seized with purpose—like a great river it began flowing south, Marden caught up in the press of bodies on its leading edge. The sound blew ahead of them, shook loose everything solid and logical and ordered, so the chaos got worse the deeper into Whitehall he was shoved. Here were all the sights he had spent his life reading about, all the landmarks, and the moment he identified them he was hustled on past.

In Hyde Park he saw his first copulating couple—a sailor with a girl straddling his waist, the two of them there in the weedy shallows of the Serpentine with a crowd cheering them on. Further on a beefy-looking sergeant held dead swans in either hand, twirled them around his head like lariats. Near Hyde Park Corner a lorry lay tipped over on its side in a circle of whisky crates, men forming a bucket brigade to distribute bottles to the crowd. On the edge of Buckingham Palace nine grim-faced soldiers faced outwards in a ring; as Marden brushed past, he saw in their middle a colonel lying on the pavement, blood streaking his ghostly white face, a private beating and stomping him with his boot as the colonel weakly raised his arm to fend him off. Bobbies stood to the side watching—bobbies stood to the side everywhere, hands clasped behind their backs, making no effort to stop anyone's fun. At the palace the crowd was so thick even the stream that had come down from Paddington could make no impression; they were brushed sideways, half running, half skipping, across the Mall. On a tree limb someone had hung an effigy of the Kaiser, and men were lined up waiting to piss on its legs. Women tore branches down, added them to a giant bonfire around which a mob stood happily singing, their faces the first he had seen showing real joy. An old man went around selling paper Union Jacks, but the price he was asking must have been too high, because a soldier stole them from him, began handing them to every pretty girl he could find. Old women, hags, rushed past with silky dresses looped around their necks—even in the loudest roar he could discriminate the sound of breaking shop windows. Between the Mall and Trafalgar Square it was impossible to find a soldier who didn't clasp a girl to his side, genteel-looking ones as well as tarts.

A bus came by, a commandeered bus, so top-heavy with passengers it listed over toward its side. They all laughed uproariously—the ones on top swayed back and forth to make it tip further, waved to those on the kerb, urging them to come join the fun. One of the conductors drove, the famous women conductors, and as she sat there, yanking the wheel this way and that, a man crouched behind her fondling her breasts. The crowd Marden was part of let out a roar. They surged forward, stopping the bus dead in its tracks, and Marden and everyone else in front was immediately shoved on. They started off along the Strand, past waving flags, people laughing, shouting and dancing, the bus windows breaking with loud crystal pops, and then just as suddenly there was another surge, and Marden found himself ejected back on the pavement again as the bus lurched away.

It was somewhat quieter in this part of the city—not a sea of humanity, but a strong, purposeful current running down the Strand. In the lull, church bells could be heard joyously pealing, the sound tossed between steeples like huge brass balls. The sun had come out, shining through the acrid-smelling dust left by fireworks; the wind blowing fresh from Piccadilly carried with it a shower of confetti. With the crowd being thinner, individual faces stood out with more distinction, so Marden could see something that until now had been thoroughly hidden. Not everyone shared the joy. There were many who didn't want any part of the celebration, had been caught out in it on their way to work or running errands, made no attempt to smile. They wore black, most of them. Black armbands, black dresses, black suits. And what's more, by an unfailing intuition they could recognize Marden as one of their own, even though he wore nothing black himself. Of all the thousands of people on these crowded streets, these were the ones his eye went to and found, and, inevitably, they would already be staring right at him, quicker than he was, more practiced, in finding grief.

Instead of letting himself be aimlessly pushed and pulled, Marden had begun making his way north toward High Holborn when he passed a pub where all the tables had been dragged outside and tipped over as a barricade. A group of young recruits drank beer from pint mugs, celebrating the miraculous fact that, against all expectation, they would live to be nineteen.

Marden, edging past the largest of the overturned tables, felt a hand grab his sleeve.

"I said, hats off, sir! Drink to the king's health, the whole bloody pitcher!"

A mug was shoved toward his throat, and when he didn't move to take it, another soldier grabbed his arm and twisted. Marden could see the taller boy was drunk, probably for the first time in his life; his face was dreamy and vicious at the same time.

"I said, drink up, sir! You a bloody Hun?"

The boy rolled his sleeves up, looked around for something to smash him with, called his mates over to watch, but just then an older, even sadder-looking civilian came past, and the recruits immediately turned their attention to him.

Another barricade down now—Marden felt this very strongly. Having been butchered so easily, never again would they give up their fun, no matter how mindless. And though he felt separated from the crowd in most respects, he could still share its overwhelming sense of liberation. No war meant no permits which meant he could go to Flanders immediately. There were taxis looking for fares, even in the thickest crowds—it would have been no trick at all to take one to the right station—but for the time being he kept on in the direction he was headed.

High Holborn turned out to be lined with cheap eating places and commercial hotels. The Adelaide sat in the middle, with a slightly larger sign and somewhat smaller windows, but in drabness just the same. All the guests must have been outside, for there was a double line along the kerb, watching as a ragged pipe band and a company of drunken guardsmen did their best to imitate a parade.

He pressed toward the entrance until he found a man alert enough to help him. The Hotel Adelaide? Someone in authority? The hotel manager? Why yes, the woman standing—well, right behind them, right there.

Mrs. Gloria was her name—she established that right off, all dignity and business, at least at first. She looked like a landlady ought to look, chiseled out of very hard stone, but drink had softened her features, and there was a sloppy good humor in her eyes that couldn't have been there very often.

"Yank, are you?" she said, when Marden introduced himself. "Lovely stuff, the Yanks. I don't care what anyone says!"

With a quicker motion than she looked capable of, she shot her hand out and grabbed his arm, brought it over to touch the hem of her dress. "Arm a stitch!" she said, laughing at her joke, told for the hundredth time that day. "Lovely, ain't it? An arm and a stitch!"

He told her who he was looking for, said the name twice before her eyes seemed to take it in.

"That little Elaine pet? Oh yes, I knew her quite well. She was here the last two nights, I think it was. Just moping about you know. Like she was waiting for"— Mrs. Gloria pointed to one of the bagpipers who had just vomited over his pipes—"peace. Like she knew it was coming. How she *knew* it was coming, that's what I keep wondering. Maybe she had a general for a gentleman friend? Had *inside* information?"

She looked him up and down, didn't bother trying to

hide her leer. "You sly roué." The phrase evidently felt so good on her tongue she said it again. "You sly roué!"

"I'm trying to find her."

"I shouldn't wonder. Some like them quiet. I'm a noisy one myself, when the moment arrives. But she's a secret one all right. A lamb really, a baby lamb. Pleasingly plump, if you fancy what I mean. Her stays a bit tight around her middle. Her cheeks getting the glow the way they do."

She clutched her head, as if the hangover were just starting. "Left, oh, it must have been an hour ago. Didn't want any part of the celebration, I noticed that much. Not much patriotic spirit if you ask me. Asked where Liverpool Street Station might be and so I told her. Didn't have a clue really about London. She set off walking with that little valise. I do so hope she makes it."

Marden thanked her for her help, but maybe she expected a tip, or couldn't resist hurling one last taunt at him, raising her voice to be heard over the bagpipes' squeal.

"I do hope it goes well, sir, the delivery. In five months' time I'll wager, judging by the swell. April. Such a good time for babies. Babies and lambs!"

❧

The taxi that stopped was decorated in bunting, but the driver was morose, complaining how peace was going to ruin his business. Afraid I was a real disappointment to him—I hardly listened. Still, he was used to reading people's expressions, and so he drove faster than was safe, up on the kerb even, weaving in and out of the mob until we reached Liverpool Street Station. Inside was as crowded as Paddington, though with a far different sort. Men and women my age, mothers and fathers, the widows again, the ones dressed in black. Most looked as though they had come suddenly; hearing of peace, they had dropped what they were doing and started off for France. A poorer sort than on ship, many women carrying parcels of food to tide them over. Never have I seen grief and eagerness melded so tightly on one mass expression. Pilgrims must look this way, praying at Lourdes.

Buy a ticket, wedge myself on. On our way east we're met by brightly lit trains coming in, as celebrants pour into London. Our separate streams cross—we exchange the yellow flicker of speeding faces, our frowns for their smiles—and then we're out in the countryside and there's nothing but dark.

Spent the ride walking from car to car, studying each person, looking for Elaine Reed. Not many young ones—it's the soldiers' parents, the older wives. Was she on another train? Is she even headed this way or has she lost courage and gone home to Wiltshire? When the landlady first told me the news I felt my heart leap in my chest, and yet I forced it back again before I could even put a name to what I felt. Now, thinking about it, I'm convinced she was lying. No one on the train who even vaguely resembled the photograph.

After five cars, I found myself looking, not for her, but for Laura. Exhaustion probably—and yet I feel envious of the fathers who have their wives to travel with. Thought of the pert, alert way Laura always sat, even on a tram, as if every journey was through Wonderland and she was a curious Alice. Said to myself—you could search a thousand cars and never find her . . . and that thought nearly did me in.

Pulled into Folkestone at midnight. Everyone climbs down onto the platform, waits until those who have been here before lead the way toward the pier. The famous embarkation town. The waterfront lined with pubs and souvenir shops, the soldiers' last chance to buy postal cards, send trinkets home, get stinko. Closed now, everything shuttered. There is nothing but the squeak of our shoes on the cobblestone, and whispered instructions when we come to a turn.

The steamer pier. Met by big sign *NO BOATS UNTIL MORNING.* Doors locked, but one big man, fists like a miner's, won't stand for it. He breaks the waiting room window, grabs the inside knob, lets the rest of us in. Everyone settles in for the night on the benches, the floor, making pillows out of their parcels, nestling against each other for warmth, no one saying a word. The station master came in five minutes ago. He looked us over, seemed on the point of ordering us out, shrugged, turned the lights down, disappeared.

As cold and hard as the bench is, for the first time since leaving home I feel—at peace? At ease? Impossible to find a word for it. Hadn't realized how alone I felt until now as the feeling slackens. Surrounded by grief, grief on all sides, and yet here I belong, right where the century wants me. In the corner, a man with a bullet-shaped head wretchedly coughs, but no one is crying, no one wails, no one sobs. And now, over everything, I can hear what sounds like a muffled drum, very distant, coming not from London but from across the Channel, like a lilting, musical kind of thunder.

❧

Marden put the diary down, extricated himself from his neighbor's shoulder, walked carefully around the sleeping forms outside. The terminal blocked the horizon, and so he walked out onto the steel pier, where the light that accompanied the sound was plainly visible in the sky eastward over France. The flashing wasn't synchronized to the thunder, but lagged a good ten seconds behind, flashing jagged before the loudest noises, scalloped before the softer ones, the color ranging from a waxy yellow to reddish black, smeared by the layer of clouds that crowned it into a bubbling, lurid jelly.

He stood there a long time watching, listening, trying to understand. Over in France gunners were celebrating midnight by letting off their cannon in a final thunderous barrage—the cause was plain enough, even to a civilian like him. The red light bubbled higher and burst, sinking back toward the yellow; the noise rose to a furious crescendo, so loud and percussive it disturbed the water along the pilings, set an inch-high wave cresting far up on shore . . . rose to its fullest crescendo, and then with a last white flash that trembled apart the clouds, it ended with him watching at the furthest edge of the pier—the war, the Great War, the last light it would ever cast.

XIV

The Channel crossing went smoothly enough, once the chaos of loading was finished. It was an old excursion steamer, the *Boadicea,* complete with calliope, side paddles and a long horseshoe bar. The cold kept most people below decks, though no food was offered. Marden took a breath of the over-used air, then went outside to find a sheltered spot where he could be alone.

The traffic was thick, considering how foggy it was. Minesweepers, hospital ships, transports. They all steamed in one direction, westward, while the *Boadicea* steamed east in the one narrow slot left open. They were happy-looking ships. Flags flew, whistles sounded, and even from the hospital ships came the slurred sound of singing.

Marden spent the first half of the voyage trying to imagine what Billy must have felt, making the same crossing. In one respect, this was easy. He would have been comparing it to crossing the strait at home, telling his mates about it, using his big, expressive hands to pantomime mountains—probably, knowing Billy, finding the Channel was in comparison a very poor thing. What else he had felt was harder to say. Would he have been proud to be going over, eager to prove himself in the oldest test the world offered young men? Or was he just fed up at that stage, bored with it all, longing already for home?

Thinking of the girl he met in Wiltshire—yes, he would be doing a lot of that. Again, Marden wondered if she was on the ship. What could she be feeling, a girl of eighteen on her first trip from home, a pregnant girl, a girl who had lost the boy she loved? The reality of the Channel, something she had heard about so often, would keep her interested for a while, as it must have Billy, as it did him. There was a childish pleasure to be had in the rippled gray surface, the brave-looking light-ships, the comic tugboats and smacks. But that wouldn't last long. What else drove her, lay deeper? He was going to Flanders to bury hope, but this wasn't what would motivate a young girl.

France came into sight quickly, a sere-colored bluff, and with the fog thinning more and more passengers found their way on deck. Space along the rail was now at a premium—there was a certain amount of jostling as people tried pressing their way forward. One man, quicker than the others, smaller, managed to slip past Marden and spread his arms possessively out over the rail.

"Pilgrims," he said, half in pity, half in contempt. "They used to travel to places where miracles were performed, now they flock to the horrors. I wonder how many will get themselves killed."

Later, when Marden got to know Roger Connor better, he would learn that this was his favorite trick— shocking you with the very first words out of his mouth. He was a short man ("Too short for the army," he would quickly explain, on every and all occasions) and perhaps this was his way of commanding attention. Marden, in that first glimpse of him, thought he was a teenage boy, and it was only when Connor turned to face him that he saw he was older, well up in his thirties, with the hard, shrewd face of a jockey, and a jockey's cockiness and bounce.

It wasn't the kind of face you needed to be gentle with. "Killed?" Marden said. "What do you mean by that?"

"Nothing has been cleaned up yet. Nothing has been prettied up or defused. I would take you for a colonel, one of the better sort. But obviously you're not. Lost a son?"

"Near Ypres. Yes."

"The Salient? Awful place . . . 'The town of Ypres lies in a natural basin formed by a maritime plain intersected by canals, dominated on the north, northeast and south by low wooded hills. The marshy ground is further soddened by constant rains and mists, which form a spongy, glutinous mass. The defense on both sides consequently centered around the woods, villages and numerous farms, which were converted into redoubts with concrete blockhouses and deep wire entanglements. The slightest bits of rising ground played an important part here, and were fiercely disputed.'"

The little man said all this in a monotone, as flawlessly as if he had notes written across his palm—so flawlessly, Marden couldn't help but smile.

"You sound like a guidebook."

"I *am* a guidebook, dear fellow. Writing one at any rate. You'll have heard of Michelin?"

"A painter?"

"The tire!"

"They're very good tires."

Connor nodded. "The finest automobile tires in the world."

Marden was to see repeated examples of this as their friendship grew—Connor was ironic on every imaginable subject *except* the quality of Michelin tires. This established, he settled back into the tone that seemed more natural to him, a mix of world-weary cynicism and patient expertise. He was writing a guidebook on the Somme and the Salient, a rush job, racing to get it out before Christmas.

"There's an enormous market," he said, spreading his arms apart. "Vast numbers of sightseers are expected, and they will all need guides."

"These aren't sightseers," Marden said.

"No, they are pilgrims. An important distinction. Sightseers will come in the next wave. Any notion how many were killed?"

Connor didn't wait for his answer. "You have to assume the official records are lies. So, let's say a million dead soldiers in England alone, speaking conservatively. Each one dead leaves two parents, so that's two million mourners at the minimum. Grieving grandparents bring the number up to four million. Wives, sweethearts—add a million more. Some had children, who won't come immediately, but they will come. Put the figure up to a safe seven million—seven million who are waiting their first opportunity to hurry over and see where their loved one got butchered. The company plans to print one hundred thousand copies just for starters."

"To sell more tires?"

Connor glanced up at him—he couldn't have been used to having his irony topped. "Ultimately—yes. But they're going to be very *good* guidebooks. Over a thousand Michelin employees died in the trenches—and that's only counting the French ones. It's not just the tires."

Connor's spirit, his refusal to accept lies, his well of information on the war—it was just what Marden needed, and he warmed very quickly to the cocky, aggressive little man. There was another delay outside Calais as they waited for a troopship to clear the harbor, and Marden surprised himself by telling him, not just about Billy, but about Elaine Reed.

Connor listened attentively, his mouth tightening into a grim alignment with the impassivity of his eyes. After four years of war, when it came to heartbreak, nothing could take that face by surprise.

"Is she aboard this ship?" he asked, the moment Marden finished. "That will have occurred to you of course. Shall we have a look? There are other boats she could have taken, from Dover or Deal, and then as you say she may have lost courage and gone home. But it's worth a chance."

They walked along the deck together, then went and made the same circuit on the starboard side, studying the faces, concentrating on the younger women, Connor, while they walked, keeping up a sotto voce recitation as to who these people were.

"Coal miners those," he said, indicating with his chin an older couple dressed in drab wool coats. "Their son probably a sapper, blown to smithereens. Padre's wife," he said, pointing to the next woman down. "Lots of them killed, the good ones who didn't funk it. Midlands those. Midlands those over there. Their sons were Kitchener boys probably. The pals battalions, all the boys from Sunday school, all the boys from the mill, joining up together, going into battle holding hands. Retired colonel that one, the pompous bastard. Stiff upper lip and all, his boy dying for his king. See how young that one? Her son probably lied about his age, recruiting boards gave a wink, and now look where it's brought her. Ah, a Bohemian! London Artists, a decent regiment. Irish that one—Tyneside Irish. And that one? Won't be a widow long, see her eyeing me, the little vixen? Probably doesn't even realize her instincts lie that way. It won't take the world long to gain back its numbers. Grandparents—see how frail? Midlands that one. Midlands her. Midlands the whole bloody lot."

One thing was certain in all this—Elaine Reed was not aboard the ship. They were entering Calais harbor now. Connor, who seemed as disappointed as Marden not to find her, came up with a fresh idea by way of consolation.

"How about motoring with me to Amiens? The company has an automobile waiting. You'll get nowhere with the trains, not without a pass. It's not Ypres, but it's not far, and once you get there you can follow the trenches northwards."

A waiting automobile? Marden was dubious, but he fell in behind him as they threaded their way down the gangway to the quay. There was confusion here, a wooden barrier that hadn't been lifted. The pilgrims, so patient until now, began pushing and shoving to get off. A French customs inspector in a short blue jacket held his hands up, blew and blew on his whistle, but it did no good. The passengers streamed around him and reformed as a solid phalanx moving purposefully toward the town's center.

Connor's automobile was waiting right where it was supposed to be—a magnificent creation, all leather, wood and brass, so large and imposing that Connor's head barely topped the tires. He proudly kicked them, looked over at Marden and winked. See? What had he been telling him? *Somptueux, non?* The driver still not appearing, he went off in search of him in the nearest café.

They returned fast enough, the chauffeur a worried-looking man in an elegant uniform. He and Connor talked rapidly, softly, in French.

"Rotten luck, I'm afraid," Connor said, coming over to where Marden waited with his bag. "I expected another driver, Jules, an excellent man. He was souvenir hunting at a place called Orvillers. The local people scavenge the battlefield. Revolvers are what they prize most, but in a pinch they'll even take helmets. Their cellars are full of them—they're stocking up for when the tourists come. Jules picked up the wrong souvenir, I'm afraid. A shell, a French seventy-five, size of a milk bottle. It blew his right hand off. Bad luck for a chauffeur."

The news seemed to sober Connor considerably. As they drove through Calais's streets, even well out into the countryside, he hardly said a word. Around them, giving way to the driver's gentle beeping, the pilgrims from the boat slowly dispersed, some to the train station, some to the taxis, some—the majority—simply walking, walking eastward, walking slowly carrying their bags and parcels, following the shadows cast ahead of them by the leaden sun.

XV

Writing this in Abbeville where we're spending our second night. Impossible delays. Had expected to be in Amiens this morning, but roads are too crowded to advance more than a few kilometers an hour. Here, rumors abound. Officers and officials chattering away in the hotel dining room over their omelettes. One rumor is that phosgene gas has seeped into the earth, and now, with the first frost, is oozing back out again, creating a cloud no one can penetrate, so the whole of eastern France is even more isolated now than it was under the Germans. Another rumor has it that the Armistice is all a ruse, the Germans are massing for an attack near St. Quentin—that all the French reservists released to their homes have been called back again by Foch.

Connor turns out to be a resourceful traveler—he's recovered some of his bounce. "Girl?" he asked, when I said goodnight. He's picked up a barmaid who has a friend. I shook my head, explained I was going for a walk. "Suit yourself," he said. "The one I found is a bit shopworn. I'm having second thoughts myself."

Had plenty of time to study the scenery today, waiting by the side of the road for our turn to advance. Soldiers made fun of our auto, whistled, spat on the brass work, rubbed it with their sleeves. Brits, marching toward the Channel ports, singing, laughing, radiating sheer animal pleasure in being alive. No Canadian boys. Connor took this in good spirit, asked them what regiments they were with, knew enough to compliment them on their stand here or their advance there. Landscape flatter than what I pictured, with little signs of war this far back. Villages can be seen from miles away, with their granaries and beet silos. Had lunch at an *estaminet* in Etaples, the hated training depot. According to Connor, this is where mutineers were shot, deserters, cowards. Looks it. A sullen place. Tattered sign on the door: *Taisez-vous les oreilles ennemies!*

Connor talks in broad terms of the war. He's well-informed, many contacts in France. Says all press accounts were total fabrications, the official communiqués outright lies. At the Somme battle, boys were sent out from the trenches wearing packs that bent them double, told to march in a straight line toward the Germans, given rum so potent nearly all of them were drunk. Twenty thousand killed in the first ten minutes, most by our own artillery, and Haig spending the entire day in bed with his Belgian mistress. And yet these were genius tactics compared to what went on near Ypres. When the full story comes out, Connor believes, there will have to be a revolution. Speaks well of the Canadians. They were the most trusted. Hard fighters like the Aussies, but more reliable, so they were in all the big shows. Their general, Currie, one of the few with brains.

This evening I took a walk along the Somme. The river is much wider here near the sea than where the battle was. Never have I seen a body of water that so perfectly lives up to its name. Somber. Somnolent. A mercurous gray color, November turned liquid. A path leading along the edge left by fishermen or cows. Three small boys in rough jerseys making boats out of tin cans. They push them encouragingly out into the current, then shell them with rocks until they sink. I walked as far as I could to where it begins curving northward, breaking up into various sluggish channels that look like dirty latrines. Walked on for a while beneath the willows, thinking about Billy, wondering where the girl is, trying to make sense of what Connor said, what happened along this river fifty miles upstream. We should be there tomorrow, if the roads are clear.

Back to the hotel. Sat for a while in the lounge drinking weak French beer the color of dandelions. Old men smoking cigars, talking, drinking. The most bizarre stories of what lies ahead.

❦

Amiens—but not without a struggle. Ten hours on the road. At first, we made good time, but by sunrise the road became blocked with masses of soldiers walking westward. Much different from what we saw the first two days. Not organized detachments, but stragglers, though even that word gives them more form than what they have. The lost ones, the confused, the dazed. Hard even determining what country they fought with. Germans in gray rags, Czechs with scarves wrapped around their heads, Portuguese, Brazilians, Chinese laborers, even Russians. Almost all are runty-looking, as if they'd spent so many years keeping their heads down they couldn't spring back again. Impossible to know how old they are. Not boys, not adults, but some separate category there is no label for. In trying to talk to them, I felt abashed like I did when I was a child talking to old men. Women, too, camp followers, though the newspapers spent the war insisting there were none of these. Some of them act like beggars, come up to us displaying their wounds, asking for money. Others are more threatening—they look like they would gladly tear the automobile in half. Our driver, I noticed, keeps a pistol beneath the rug on his seat. Connor says there are organized gangs living in No Man's Land, killing and stealing to survive, raiding the local villages for women, turning cannibal. One man, an officer, an amputee, waves his crutch at us, screams incomprehensibly, and the chauffeur guns the motor to get around. On the rises, so flat is the land, we could see the road for miles ahead, and it looked to be moving, as if all these stragglers carried the paving stones on their back.

Connor gave some francs to one of the boys. When our driver objected to this, Connor screamed at him in fury. The soldier he gave it to—was he even sixteen?—was a sad enough case. He had on a Yank helmet, British webbing, German boots, and must have been a Russian prisoner, a Siberian, an Eskimo, with the lonely sled dog look I remember from my time in the north.

We stopped at an *estaminet*—Connor drank well down into a bottle of *vin ordinaire*. He kept asking me questions about what I deal with on the island, the petty crime, the wife beatings, the brawls. I thought he was changing the obvious subject.

"No," he said. "There's a connection, there must be. Someone horsewhips a bully in the arctic frontier you dwell in and here in France the same impulse leads to sixty thousand boys being shot in ten minutes. How else can you explain the criminal agreements the allies made to parcel up the smaller countries? How else can you explain German aggression?"

"You know I don't credit any of that," I said. "Your politics. The great game. It has nothing to do with this at all."

"Of course not. Quite right. Childish stuff really. But listen here, Marden. If Austria had shown even slightly more restraint . . ."

Amiens turns out to be a thoroughly bourgeois city, showing little in the way of damage. Yes, shell holes in many buildings, but they look harmless, like mice have been nibbling at the walls. Avenue V. Hugo. Avenue Jeanne D'Arc. Avenue Pasteur. Many families, the ones who funked it, returning home now. Laborers move gilt-framed paintings and mahogany furniture back indoors. Passed a lorry full of heavily rouged women barreling down the Paris road. "Whores," Connor said, giving them a wave. "Off to search for another war."

And we've caught up with the influenza again, or it's caught up with us. Gauze masks. Squads going around with disinfectant, which they squirt on everything, even the petals of old rose bushes that line the squares. They don't hide death here, or have become weary of doing so. We passed a stockpiled pyramid of coffins on our way in, many of them quite small.

❧

Had a dream in which pain and sweetness were wound so tightly around each other it was like a rope tied in an overhand knot around my heart. And it was backwards, the logic. The afternoon of our wedding. Laura's friends and relations were gathered in the front parlor, crying, because the wedding had all been a charade, and everyone knew they were really gathered there to mourn her death. Her kindly Aunt Alice, her mother and sisters, that hatchet-faced cousin who had been so cruel to her when she was small. And a young Billy was there, too, his face red with indignation and impotent fury, that everyone insisted on being sad when he knew she was still alive. He runs from the room, dives cleanly into the sea upon which the parlor is floating, and no one notices he is gone but me. I feel guilty over this, want to scream from quilt's unbearable weight. It comes in iron bars delivered by messengers who lay it directly on my chest.

The relatives continue talking—I could hear this with perfect clarity—about Laura's hands. Realistic enough, that part. Everyone always talked about Laura's hands. How beautiful they were, how delicate, the implication being they were too fragile to be given into the care of a brute like me and taken away to the wilderness. That was the worst part of the dream, my yelling at them they were wrong. If they had seen the way she took to the work in the orchard or in her garden, felt the strong loving pressure of those hands on my back on our nights alone, seen the way she went at her painting, not delicately, but boldly, her fingers firm on the brush and sure. . . .

I told them this in the dream, woke from it sweating, then lay there continuing the argument as you do when you're shaken. My evidence was the night Billy was born, that wild September midnight of gale winds and sleet and shattered windows, and only Margaret Cooper there to help us. The agonizingly long ordeal. Laura's hands in mine, me trying to do the best I could for her by matching her pressure, squeezing when she did, keeping up with the spasms. But then suddenly she drew back from me, the pain was too intense now, and I couldn't help. Margaret behind us, calm, unflappable, or so I thought—and then I looked around and she was sobbing, too, helpless, at least for that one terrible moment, and now I understood this wasn't a normal part of it, that things were very bad. Then, that very moment, Laura swaying toward me again, putting her hands around behind on my back—no, not her hands, but her *fists,* so they dug deep into my flesh and hurt. Fists, not hands. Tightened fists, the bunched sharp knuckles so hard on my back it was all I could do not to yell. But I realized even then that those fists were holding in the pain it was impossible for her to share, what she had to go through alone—and somehow she had to signal this to me from as deep in solitude as a woman could descend to and still manage to return. Her little clenched fists were where her humanity lay, her courage, and she was pressing them into my back because she wanted to give *me* courage, signal that she had grasped strength at that supreme moment, and, what's more, had enough left over to send it via this pressure on to me.

Later, talking to Margaret, trying to explain what I had felt, I found she already knew from all her experience nursing about this business with fists and what they held of a soul. Old people who had always hated life, she told me, inevitably died with their hands open, limp and flat. Old people who had always loved life—and she had never seen an exception to this—died with their hands tightly clenched.

There was no death, not on that night. When Laura's fists relaxed there was this impossibly small being there before us, seemingly conjured out of her hands, this being the miracle of childbirth everyone kept secret. And Billy. Born with his hands clenched—I saw that immediately—and the very first time I held him, the very first thing I ever did for him, was to wedge my little finger gently between his fingers, and take that instinctive clutching pressure straight into my heart.

☙

Marden was left to his own devices the next day, as Connor went to work. There were hotels he had to visit to see if they were still functioning, courtesy calls to make on Michelin officials, fact checking to do in town before trying the roads to the front lines. Marden walked alone to the city center, asked at the rail station for information about going north. By train it was a complex affair, requiring a multitude of passes, but there was a bus to Bruges in the morning, the first since the war ended, and Ypres lay along its route.

It was late afternoon before Connor returned to the hotel. "In the mood for some climbing?" he asked, mysteriously enough.

It was the cathedral he led him to, the very last place Marden was in the mood to visit. Instead of using the main entrance, Connor took him around the side to an intricately carved, very narrow wooden door. A monk waited there to open it for them; as usual, Connor seemed to have everything arranged.

"Watch your head here," he said, tapping his own. "There are steps to begin with, but then it's mostly a question of ladders."

The monk wore a thick woolen cowl puckered

around his head, and the only thing visible of his face was a mask over his mouth that seemed made of the same material. He went first up a damp passageway that led from the warm scent of incense to the dank smell of mold. High above in a narrow shaft was a thin crescent of sunlight, and this is what they climbed toward, step by laborious step. Even the monk gave up when they came to the ladders; his arm emerged from the robe and gestured upwards in a final despairing benediction.

Connor was small and lithe enough to climb fairly quickly, but his nerves were bad—he stopped frequently to rest. One of these pauses was beside a bell so coated in pigeon droppings it couldn't have rung in several centuries. Connor had a silver flask in his pocket, and, after taking a big swig, he politely handed it over.

"Need some steadying? This last bit is a bit more worrisome than what we've done."

The ladder led through an opened trap door into a square vaulted chamber only an inch or two higher than the top of Marden's head. It was hard to discern its purpose. Had it once been a watchtower, a dovecote, a prison? There were shuttered windows, one in each compass direction. Connor, using the filtered sunlight as his guide, went over to the east-facing one and heaved open its shutter.

The wind poured in on their faces with the force of a hard slap. Marden's eyes teared immediately. It was an acrid wind, not just a cold one, carrying with it fumes from every chimney in the city. Squinting, staring down, he could make out a pinwheel of slate-roofed buildings looped by the Somme, looking even grayer and more sluggish here than it had back in Abbeville, like a dirty bandage that had fluttered down from the cathedral's spires.

The river view was not why Connor had brought him there. He stood behind him now, pointed eastward. The window was high enough to see a long way into the Picardy countryside, with the setting sun magnifying the detail. What it spotlighted was a vaguely undulating series of muddy fields, with no discernible logic or trend to the elevation—it was like a pudding with random lumps. And yet, right from that first glimpse, it struck Marden with a force that was as hard and sharp as the wind's—the realness of it, the actuality. It was like having heard of heaven and hell, and finding out, in one revelatory moment, that this is what they consisted of—not magic zones of fire, not fleecy layers of clouds, but a vaguely undulating series of muddy fields that looked like a lumpy pudding.

"*Voilá*," Connor said, smiling ironically. "The Western Front."

The lumpy brown fields, Marden saw now, were crossed with suture-like lines, some of them peat-colored, others putty-colored, others the color of old ivory. Clay, he decided, after staring for a time. Excavated clay, shoveled and tossed, dried now, hardened. These sutures, these low mounds, went everywhere, some lying parallel to the horizon, others running perpendicular; even the straightest were cut with zigzags, like bites made by a dragon who couldn't make up his mind which way to chew.

"Communication trenches," Connor said, following

his eyes. "They were dug crooked like that to prevent enfilade fire if raiding parties got into a trench. See the shiny stuff? Right, squint again."

It was a gossamer flashing he saw at first, with a wet look, so it was like seeing a spider's web first thing in the morning. Only as the sun dropped could he make out the hard metallic flash of it, a taunting kind of twinkle, and realized what he was looking at was belt after belt of barbed wire.

All the peat-colored mounds, the ivory-colored seams, were matched in the distance by a color of exactly the same blend, with a similar glaze over it, similar flashings. The German front line, the German second line, the German third line—he didn't need Connor's explanation. What seemed like vertical chunks of charcoal were the remains of woods and forests. The lumps in the pudding were blockhouses and redoubts. The raisins were ruined churches or chateaus. The yellow-pink stain on the edge of the clay was what happened to earth under poison gas.

As the view fell into place, began making sense, he felt a surprise that shook him even harder than the first jolt had—how thin a line this was, how small the space involved, how unbelievable to think that the fate of civilization had come to depend on these few puny acres.

Back on the island he had a friend named Andre Slater who had a farm and grew potatoes. It wasn't a particularly big farm, not by western standards, and yet the battlefield he stared at could have fit inside with room to spare. In the end, it was this comparison that defeated him—thinking how many boys had died trying to cross Andre Slater's farm.

"Marden?"

He couldn't bear staring and he couldn't bring his head away—the vice tightened no matter which way he looked. There was a cold sensation against his hand, the flask with the cognac, Connor pressing it toward him.

"That's Longueval toward the left. Montauban further left. The Bapaume Road, what's left of it. Mametz and La Boiselle."

Connor kept up a steady recitation, stopping only to take another swallow from the flask. But this was absurd of him, insane. There was nothing to point to, no villages, no towns. He was grabbing handfuls of air, empty vapor, christening it with names.

"That saucer there, the one with a rust-colored circumference? The mine crater at Beaumont Hammel. You'll have heard of that."

Marden looked to where he pointed. It was as if the earth, weary everywhere, was even more exhausted inside the rusty circle and had simply collapsed.

The crater seemed to be the end of Connor's little tour. He sat down on a bulge in the stonework, leaned his head back at an odd angle until his cheek was flush with the wall.

"This"—he waved his hand out—"will all be in a guidebook someday. That's all it will be—lines in a guidebook. The Rifle Brigade marched bravely toward Orvillers. The plucky Newfoundlanders stormed the Schwaben Redoubt, the outlines of which are still clearly discernible in the clay. Nothing matched the gallantry of the Anzacs near Fricourt."

Marden glanced down at him. "Then you had better make it a good guidebook."

"Oh, I will. Rest assured of that, Marden. Starting tomorrow. I'll take a week to explore, two weeks even." He reached down, tapped his shoes. "I need to feel it under my feet."

He was in a queer mood, it was hard to know whether he was being cynical or sincere. He didn't say anything for a time, but stared gloomily out the little chamber, sipping at his flask. Marden went back to the window, looked down past the gargoyles and the buttresses to the Somme. A stubby, plow-shaped barge was making its way downriver, spreading the water apart in a slow, muddy V.

"And do you know," Connor said, as if he had kept talking to himself during the silence, "my plan would be this, if I were in charge of this century. I'd bring one man here to try and make sense of all this. Just one man, to avoid disputation. Not a young man either—someone your age—but from a young country. Not a city man, but someone used to seeing nature at its best. A judge—someone who can size things up, deal with thorny issues. A thoughtful man, not a talker. Someone with good eyes, deep eyes, eyes that miss nothing."

The barge veered in toward the embankment, slowed, the V widening out until it lost its shape.

"I wonder, Marden, wondered ever since I met you. Your eyes, your manner, the few words I pry from you. It's made me harbor a terrible suspicion."

"Which is?"

"Do you know everything there is to know about man?"

Only now did Marden turn and look down at him.

He smiled, or tried to. "Do you know everything there is to know about—this?"

Connor tapped the flask, held it sadly upside-down. "No," he said. "But I will."

He got up from his bench, took the three steps needed to cross the chamber, stood leaning against the opposite shutter, facing Marden but not looking at him directly.

"People think small men are brave to make up for their smallness. Lloyd George, the Tiger of Wales. Clemenceau, the Tiger of France. Even that bastard Foch . . . It's not true, Marden. It's simply not true. I felt all during the war that it was my fate to die here. Not necessarily on the Somme, but along the front, maybe near Ypres like your son, or maybe at Mons or Vimy Ridge. I had a strong premonition. Right then, friends said, those I confided in. What a lucky thing, your premonition. You can avoid it, duck conscription like you've been doing . . . What they didn't understand is that fate is fate, that you can't escape it just because it's polite enough to give you a warning tap on the shoulder. How many boys, serving out there, felt a tap on their shoulders? They all did, but how many avoided it in the end? . . . All right. I'm sounding morbid. You must be used to that, being the kind of judge you are. People want to confess to you, test whether those eyes can deliver on their promise."

A clump of dust fell from the chamber's beam, a second ahead of the loud pealing of the cathedral bells signaling vespers. The bell tower was below the chamber, that was what was strange about it—to be standing

above church bells, with the sound, the tintinnabula-
tions, coming through their feet.

It pulled Connor back from whatever he teetered on.
"You're off tomorrow?" he asked, all trace of agitation
gone.

Marden told him about the bus. Connor nodded,
reached into his pocket for a pad, scribbled a name
down, tore the page off, handed it over.

"I want you to look up Monsieur Brunfaut in Ypres.
The local Michelin agent. He used to be mayor, stuck it
during the worst of the shelling—there's nothing he
can't help you with. He's a good man, Marden. Like
yourself."

Marden nodded, put the paper in his wallet.

"There are hotels in Poperinghe that will suit you.
Close enough to the front line for exploring, I expect.
You'll find nothing in Ypres but ruins. I'll be along
myself when I finish here."

XVI

The driver of the bus expected to be welcomed as a lib-
erator. He had decorated the windows with bunting,
dressed in his best blue uniform, stuck hothouse flowers
in every crack. The passengers caught his mood—this
was the first bus to Flanders in almost four years. But
there was nothing triumphant about their journey. The
French peasants, wary in the best of circumstances, had
learned during the war that anything mechanized could
only bring sorrow, and so there was no welcome for
them in any of the villages, the only ones out on the

street being young boys who hurled clods of dung at the bus and darted in to strip away the flowers.

The route they followed detoured west around the front and only approached it again crossing the border into Belgium. It was a surprisingly tranquil corner with little sign of war, and it gave Marden time to get his thoughts in order before reaching the Salient—to concentrate on Billy, not remembering any specific scenes, but how much delight he had taken over the years in watching the growth of his intelligence, so much quicker than his own, so much more intuitive, requiring none of the hard puzzling he needed before coming up with an answer himself. The island had poor schools, taught by men who could find no other work. But Billy wasn't the kind who needed schools; in his hands, in his eyes, was a sureness that needed no help. Marden was proud of this—of course he was proud. And yet leaving that aside, he recognized that Billy was the kind of boy who, coming to manhood, could help the world leap ahead by sheer imaginative pulling.

But even this sense of him, general as it was, slipped away inside the Salient. No individual memory, no specific scene, could withstand the weight of what had happened there. He felt this the moment the bus came into Poperinghe and deposited him in the central plaza—that an iron shutter had dropped between him and his son's memory, and that from now on his mission was, not just to see where he had been killed, but to lift the shutter, bore through it back to the memory of Billy, not as a soldier of the king, not as another digit in the wretched mass of digits in Connor's guidebook, not as just another young man turned under by history's plow, but as William Cooper Marden, his son, his only boy.

He wondered if Elaine Reed felt anything like he did—what memories she reached for herself. There couldn't have been many. Their first meeting, the way Billy had approached her booth at the fair. Playing it over and over in her mind, the moment she first saw him step out from the circle of soldiers, the first second she saw him alone, distinctly, not just as part of the dizzying carnival blur everything seemed caught up in. His climbing Cromwell's Oak as she laughed and applauded. Their afternoon walk along Sommers Lane, lying in the meadow, the memory so sweet and intense it was impossible to focus on, though she tried again and again. This would all seem like a dream of course. Even the child at this stage. Even the strengthening heartbeat she could feel with her hand.

He was sure from that very first moment that Elaine Reed was somewhere inside the Salient—that searching for Billy now meant searching for her. There was no hard evidence for this, nothing definite, not at first. But the Salient, he quickly discovered, was a place of portents, omens and premonitions, a hundred times stronger inside than out. And why shouldn't it be? The border between life and death had been drawn more thinly along the front than anywhere else, at any time, so communication across that border, if possible anywhere, was possible there. He had always been a skeptic when it came to spiritual messages, but moments after descending from the bus in Poperinghe he became a convert, to the deepest part of his being.

The moment, that is, when waiting in the endless

queue of pilgrims hoping for a room, striking up a conversation with the toothless old Cockney couple next to him, the very first people he had spoken to in Flanders, asking them, as he would eventually ask everyone, whether they had seen a girl of her description on their long walk up from Calais, the man looked at his wife, rubbed his ears, brought it out.

"Girl from Wiltshire? Bashful-looking sort, pretty, with a certain set to her eyes? Why Lilly, we saw her when, two days ago? We saw her hoofing it along the road from that Steenvoorde place, looking like she was having a hard go of it, being with child that way, and so I carried her bag for her, oh, it must have been a mile before Lilly's ankles began to swell the way they do and we had to stop while she thanked us and went on."

XVII

Found a room in the attic of the Café de Ranke. "Ginger's" it's called, for the three redheaded daughters of the proprietor. They're famous, or act like it, and yet they must sense their celebrity days as darlings of the officers are over now, with nothing left for them but to lose what's left of their looks. The room was small, not much wider than the bed, and yet how wonderful it must have felt to boys coming out of the line, the clean sheets, the linen. Slept like they must have, blissfully grateful.

Up early. The sun too weak to penetrate the mist, only it wasn't mist, but a cloying kind of dust. As I stood there outside the town hall, pilgrims began emerging from the various rooming houses and hotels, alone at first, then in twos and threes, the groups merging, milling aimlessly about, directionless, so they seemed awaiting orders to march. Wooden brewery vats still line one side of the plaza—where the soldiers were taken for baths. For lack of anything better to look at, pilgrims wander over to these, get up on tiptoe to peer inside, rub their fingers around the rims.

A long trestle table set up near the fountain, a great steaming kettle, women in shawls and sabots standing there with bowls ready to serve anyone who's hungry. Fine idea, I thought—the authorities must realize the numbers they're dealing with—but then, moving closer, I found it was run by a local man who saw his chance to make a killing. A crude sign, *Eggs! Fish! Chips! Tea!* Most of the pilgrims took a look at his prices, shrugged, walked back to the center of the plaza, opened the parcels they had brought from home.

Staggering, the numbers. Hundreds, I guessed, but then more kept coming, joined by those who had spent the night in villages to the west, until there must have been a thousand or more crammed into the plaza outside the Stadhuis, people my age, having the eager, anxious look parents have when they go to a party to fetch home their child.

It was the sun that finally took charge, got us moving. It rose high enough to yellow up the dust, create the illusion of warmth—rose in the east, and eastward we started to walk. There was no command, no leader. Between the allure of the sun, the sheer press of pilgrims, the narrowness of the streets, our mass was squeezed into a column, two columns, and these columns began walking slowly along the slick, high-cambered cobblestones of the Ypres Road.

Our way led across a flat plain past withered hop fields, the poles used to hold them up slanting sideways in the mud like a forest of spears. There were no autos or carts on the road, not at first. No one came from the other direction, no soldiers, no stragglers, no wounded—everyone is gone now from the Salient who is capable of leaving. At the crossroads, local people went about their business, hardly gave us a glance. The women in long black skirts, muddy sabots, black stockings, the men wearing aprons that made them look like their wives. Approaching Vlamertinghe, a village curé in his heavy boots and vast soutane took off his broad-brimmed hat and stood with his head bowed as we marched past.

Most walked in silence, but some needed to talk. I flanked a man named Lockey whose son was in the Notts and Derbyshire regiment, the ones known as the Sherwood Foresters. A tall mill hand with muscular eyebrows, proud of his son who was commissioned from the ranks. What happened to his boy is this. The battalion was in rest behind the lines. Bored, a group of four officers including his son went to watch the first tanks practicing their maneuvers in a muddy field. The tank crews were new, they could hardly control their machines, the tank in the lead trampled down all four of them and crushed them beneath its treads. The official letter said he'd been killed leading an advance, and it was only a frank letter from his sergeant that contained the truth.

After this came a man and a woman, older, poorer,

carrying nothing with them but their natural dignity and decency. Their son a corporal who was gassed near Hooge. Not German gas, but British. Readying gas for an attack, the wind from the wrong direction, the boys so drunk on rum they couldn't decide how to open the canisters. They opened them, phosgene began blowing back on the British trench, their son volunteered to go and close the spigots at the cost of his life. Again, this was given to them quietly, by an invalid pal back in Britain who wanted them to know.

Every hour, by what seemed a spontaneous agreement, we sat down on the cobblestones to rest, our feet dangling toward the ditch running along the road's edge. At one of these stops a bespectacled man in a tweed suit carrying a walking stick went from person to person, stooping down to hand them something, then sadly pulling it back again before repeating the action with the next one along.

My turn came. He looked like a don, an Oxford don, with the owl-like eyes, the harried manner. What he handed me was a framed photograph of a boy in uniform who looked just like him.

"Have you seen him?" he asked, his voice so hoarse I could barely make it out. "My son Robin. Lost near Hollebeke, reported missing. Queens Westminster Rifles. You're not a soldier, yes I understand, but I must ask you. I must ask everyone."

I shook my head. He stepped across my legs to the next person down. "My son Robin. Have you seen him?" and so on along the line.

One striking thing. Most can't put into words why it is they've come. Visiting the proper cemetery, saying goodbye. Yes, partly. But it must be something more than this, the lodestone that tugs, something strong enough to make them leave home immediately. Lockey for instance. His boss at the mill wouldn't hear of it, his leaving, so he up and quit. And then many of them carry parcels with them, tins of biscuit and cocoa, extra clothing beyond what they need for themselves. This struck me hardest, though I was slow to understand. There is not one of these people, not one, who truly believes their boy is dead. We've come, we've all come, to warm them, feed them, fetch them home.

Eight miles to Ypres, seems much longer. We were nearing the city, though it remained out of sight, when a big touring auto roared past, people hurrying to the sides to get out of its way. Two couples riding behind the chauffeur—the women with short hair, makeup, the men wrapped in fur coats pulled up around their ears. Tourists, the first I've seen. One of the women points a Brownie at me, snaps a picture. The pilgrims move out of the automobile's way, re-form behind it, keep walking. Many of these are tired, footsore, weary. Why don't they commandeer the auto, toss its occupants into the ditch? Stupid question. For the same reason we let our sons be chewed apart by machines.

A few minutes later our column slowed even more. Hop fields on the side and there in the mud a single long groove, like a giant had gone sliding nose first just for fun. A shell hole, the first we've seen, enough of a curiosity that people stop and point. A hundred yards along we came upon another groove, this one deeper, leading to an actual crater covered with a sudsy brown froth, as if the giant had scooped out a bath. At the same time, I noticed the stakes in the field, the ones holding up the hop vines, weren't stakes at all, but shattered trees, sharp as knives, the stumps blackened and seared.

After six or seven of these craters no one bothered to stop. There came a blistered sign, *Tin Hats Must Be Worn From This Point Onwards*—nicely placed, since now, one either side of the road, the craters, the shell holes, were continuous, forming an overlapping series of shit-colored saucers. And yet the real front, No Man's Land, was still six miles distant.

Outside Vlamertinghe stood a barrel-chested civilian acting like he was taking charge and those who didn't like it could damn well do as they pleased. What he had taken charge of was a collection of artillery shells that had been piled beside the road. In their color, in the harmless way they lay there, they resembled a stack of pulp logs waiting to be rolled into a river.

"Duds," the man walking beside me said, pointing.

At that, the self-appointed guard snorted in contempt. "Duds! Those ain't duds! One of these beauties went off and killed a bloke from Hull just this morning. Yes, and another went off yesterday, spun around a lady from Blackpool like she was waltzing and took off her arm!"

Ahead of me, the road swelling higher, I spotted a girl who was the youngest I'd seen yet, judging by her slenderness, the quick eager way she walked. Long hair— she wore no hat. Somehow I convinced myself it was Elaine Reed—that she was walking there ahead of me not fifty yards away. My heart started beating even before I began running. I dodged around the pilgrims in front of me, shoved some of the men to clear a path, was just on the point of calling out her name, when I saw her suddenly stop and just stand there staring at something which, gaining the crest now, I still couldn't see.

I caught up to her. I stood beside her, saw her glance over her shoulder in my direction . . . a full-faced girl, older than she looked from the distance, sadness smeared across her face with rouge . . . and then, before my disappointment could even form, she turned back again, and I looked toward what she was staring at.

Ypres—and yet I thought I was looking at cloud. Like the ruined city was cloud, the same consistency and color. Broken cloud. Cloud that had been ripped and hacked apart, so all the fluidity and softness had leaked out, and what was left was jagged and sharp, cloud that hurt. Behind the cloud was a crenellated silhouette, like distant mountains, and it required hard staring to resolve this into buildings, the remains of buildings. Pointing toward them, closer, were more of the dagger-like trees we had seen earlier, pinning the cloud to earth. The smell of wet plaster was overpowering, only now there was an oily smell that went with it, so it was impossible to draw a breath without gasping. Everyone stared—you could look all the way down the road and see pilgrims turned the same way, held by that gap-toothed silhouette, the beaten clouds, the jagged ruins.

It was hard to get moving again. The destruction was so total it made it seem we were children walking a long plank over the abyss. Men and women, those who were together, spontaneously held hands, and it caught on, some of the women taking the hands of strangers next to them, these phlegmatic Britishers who ordinarily wouldn't do anything of the kind. A long chain, making me think of the pictures I'd seen of gassed men, blinded men, holding each other's shoulders as they tramped back from the front.

It was in just such a line that we entered Ypres.

XVIII

Writing this on a wooden shutter propped between a porcelain commode and a brass spittoon, the abandoned treasures of a ruined villa. I'm in the garden, what used to be the garden, in a miniature fortress made by the collapse of its walls. Morning now, after a sleepless and hallucinatory night.

It was nearly dusk when we came into the city through the tunnels of debris, but even to call it "debris" suggests more shape than these ruins have. Most are powder, an incredibly fine powder, knee-high dunes of it, spreading everywhere. The only things higher are the remains of the ancient Cloth Hall—once as lavish, built with as much grace and care, as a cathedral. What's left now is a huge, purple-black pile that looks like the slag heap of a coal mining town, and atop this a blocky tower that seems constructed of pure dust. Running back at an angle is a broken wall with vaulted windows, or holes where these windows had been, a double layer of chalky white matter that seems only one stage thicker than pure air. Telegraph poles reeking of creosote prop all this up, the butts wedged into the ground for purchase. The arches, the vaults, seem existing by sheer magic; you can stare at them for a long time and not understand how they sustain their shapes. It's as if four years of shelling have left behind a glutinous material made specifically to bind destruction together, not allow it to slide into a decent heap that could then be swept away. If you stand back, try to take everything in at once, the ruins look like the long white jawbone of a mule, with the teeth chipped and splintered, the bone either cracked or shot away.

The pilgrims milled around as it grew dark, pointing, shaking their heads, reaching down now and again to pluck something recognizable from the debris. A comb, a bottle, a toy. Most of them hadn't realized the destruction is so total here—most of them thought they could find a hotel room as in any other city. It's too far to walk back to Poperinghe, though I could see some start down the road doing just that. A Belgian woman has a stand where she sells blankets. German blankets, she assured everyone. Made in Hamburg, twelve francs each. The implication was clear. If you weren't up to walking twelve miles back to Poperinghe, you had to find yourself a hole to spend the night.

Past the Cloth Hall is a street where the debris lies further apart than on the other streets, giving it a bizarre note of gentility. A sign splashed with blue lettering advertises *Singer Nähmaschinen.* This must be where the old wall that encircled the city was, for the house I found, the remains of the house, lies against a massive stonework façade, creating a network of catacombs and sheds. I wasn't the first one using this—the garden dirt had been dug away to make a deep hole. Soldiers before me? Desperate civilians?

As I settled into my cave, a man and woman settled into theirs. We talked hole to hole. They're from Liverpool, spoke so fast, with such accents, it was hard understanding. It's their daughter who died, a VAD nurse who came to Ypres in search of a friend of her brother's who had been wounded in the big push of 1917. She had gone against standing orders making Ypres off-limits— a plucky girl, and it was her pluck that did for her, killed by a German shell that landed on the train station. Buried, according to what they've been told, in the British cemetery behind the insane asylum, and they spent all afternoon searching for it in the maze of rubble. They asked if I knew where it might be, and I promised to help them as soon as it was morning . . . but now it is morning and there's no sign of them, they've already gone. "We must live for the future," the woman told me just before dark when they came over for a visit. She said this several times. Her husband nodded for her sake without believing.

An odd lingering twilight. Whoever occupied this hole before me left behind a stub of candle, and thanks to a match from my neighbors I managed to get it burning. Enough for the illusion of warmth at any rate. I thought of all the others crouched in similar holes, knew they were thinking the same thing I was for consolation—well, no matter how bad this is, my boy faced worse. Between the bread I carried from Poperinghe and a stick of chocolate given me by the man whose son died turning off the gas, I managed something like dinner, then, pulling the German blanket up around my shoulders, settled in to see what the night would bring.

For a while I could hear muffled talking, not only

from my neighbors' hole, but from the others nearby. And peeing—men relieving themselves against the ruined wall. And hammering—someone making himself right at home. But as the night thickened, the sounds faded away, and everything became silent enough that the air, the part of air that supports sound, seemed to turn over, change sides, producing a different kind of silence altogether.

A difficult notion to pin down. It was as if the silence smothered all normal sounds and supported extraordinary ones you had to use all your wits to decipher. The first was a grainy scratching similar to what you would get if you rubbed your fingers over coarse paper. Soft, but irritating. And a sifting kind of sound, like sand running down a dune. The sound, I finally decided, of pulverized plaster settling deep within the mounds of debris. Atop this came louder noises—the woody groans of beams bending underneath the debris, then actual reports as they snapped.

I spent all night with this, watching, listening, sleeping for ten minutes, then sitting bolt upright. It started raining after midnight—a steady trickle as rivulets found each other, joined forces, ran down my neck. I struggled to make sense of what I was hearing. The sifting sounds were swollen with dampness, but as far as I could determine all originated here within the city's walls. And yet at the same time they spread outwards like ripples, hit something solid in the distance, bounced back again totally transformed. I could hear dogs yipping, a pack of dogs, then a hacking, coughing sound I couldn't account for. A noise like thunder, only without the echo, coming as bursts of compressed air that bore in on my eardrums and made them throb. *Whump whump whump.* It was as if one sound ignited the next right along a line. With this came a softer, more sibilant sound—*phew phew phew.* I remembered the stories I'd heard back in Abbeville about deserters living in No Man's Land, raiding the surrounding villages. Were these gunshots theirs? Or is it just that the front is littered with so much ammunition, artillery shells, bullets, that they don't need anything to set them off, that even a rat, treading on a detonator, could get them going?

Or ghosts—the woman in the next hole talked about them and her husband tried laughing her off. I think he was wrong in this, that there is something in what she said. The word itself didn't frighten me. If anything, I sensed a bitter rightness in the notion. Why not ghosts? Give boys such weapons, fill their heads with lies, stuff them with hate, and why shouldn't they continue fighting even dead?

Go ahead and fight then, I thought, as the night wore on. Now, with no one watching, go ahead and fight.

XIX

In the morning, finished with his diary, Marden went in search of Monsieur Brunfaut.

The pilgrims were awake now, climbing out of their shelters and holes, looking shabbier than they had the day before, less purposeful. They acted, Marden decided, like men and women whose future had been stolen from their pockets while they slept. Their foreheads seemed too heavy and their spines too soft, as if they couldn't find even the minimum expectancy needed to face the coming day. The wells still worked, and the women stood waiting their turns to dip their heads under the thin streams that dripped from the spouts. Many of them held something round and fragile-looking under the water, and it was only when he joined the queue himself that he realized that these were floral wreaths, carried tenderly from England, needing water now, on the point of drying out.

At least it was warm—warmer than what you could expect in November. The sun, rising above the ruined Cloth Hall, heated the debris enough that it gave off a thin greenish steam. And commerce was returning to the city, of a sort. There were trestle tables set up selling food, doing good business, and the blanket woman was joined by others selling knitted sweaters and socks. One man offered souvenirs—helmets, swords, pistols. Business was slow, but he didn't seem bothered by this; he stood there whistling, rising up and down on the balls of his feet, confident, knowing his turn would come.

The Michelin garage was on what remained of the rue des Chiens. A path had been punched through the middle of the debris, just wide enough that an automobile could pass. Where the tunnel ended were four autos parked beside a metal shed that was by far the newest, cleanest building Marden had seen. A man stood outside, a man made of pneumatic tires, with thin ones for legs, fat ones for a stomach, and, on top, a rubber head with racing goggles for eyes. *Entrez!* read the sign around his neck. The biggest of the autos was the one Marden had seen yesterday, the touring model that had nearly run the pilgrims off the road. Its front end was smashed—one of the tires was missing. The windscreen was shattered, too, and there were deep, finger-sized gouges in the leather seats.

A woman sat inside the shed, framed by limp tires that hung down from pegs, scribbling furiously across a yellow pad, her head wagging so fast it made the tires tremble. She was dressed in black, as was everyone in the Salient, only on her it didn't seem like mourning, but the color that best highlighted her fierceness. Madam Brunfaut, he assumed. She was intelligent and shrewd-looking, and she hardly glanced up at him at all.

"*Demain,*" she said impatiently. "*Demain!*"

Marden, with what French he remembered from his boyhood, asked for her husband.

She looked up at him now, in a way that surprised him—without hardness, but in fear.

He'd gone to Amiens, she explained. Gone there yesterday on urgent company business. He was supposed to be back by nightfall, but he hadn't returned. God knows why this was so. There were many things that could happen, especially at night. Many things. She snapped her fingers—the sound was startling. The English snapped their fingers and announced the war was over, and yet it wasn't over, not for those who still lived here.

I'm not English, Marden said, smiling gently. The woman looked him up and down. All the better for you, she said.

She followed him to the door. "*Où sont les touristes?*" he asked, pointing to the ruined car.

She understood him, he was sure of that, but without

answering she turned on her heel and disappeared inside.

Marden, somewhat at a loss, followed the tunnel of the road eastward through the remains of the Menin Gate. Other pilgrims walked in the same direction, but nothing like the solid stream he had been part of yesterday. Almost immediately, he came to a crater in the center of the broken cobblestone, with men and women standing on the lip peering down. One man, the oldest, tossed pebbles toward the heavy, sherry-colored scum on the bottom. People watched as the ripples disappeared; gradually, shyly, they turned to ask each other the way to this cemetery or that, comparing notes, pulling out impossibly vague maps, trying to make sense of where they were.

Marden did his own asking. One man, with more of a military bearing than the others, pointed toward the southeast, thought Gheluvelt might lie out there, though he warned Marden that once you got a quarter mile from the city every road became impassable, and it was suicide to take a shortcut and travel cross-country.

"Gas is worst," he said, clutching his hand around his throat. "The phosgene. A warm day like this, there in the trenches, you can see it start in to bugger and boil."

The road quickly rose out of its tunnel and became even with the plain. Marden could see a good distance, not only back to the crenellated line made by the Ypres ruins, but a considerable distance to the north and east, the Salient's heart. Again, trying to make sense of it, he thought of the sea—the sea during a tumultuous storm, where the wind and current worked at cross purposes, churning up steep pyramids at one place and deep furrows just beyond . . . the sea, only dried, frozen, desiccated, so all these shapes stood still.

A low purple weed clung to the smoother furrows, but it was tougher-looking than the dirt, and did nothing to relieve the overall gloom. There was no sign of poppies, the famous red poppies, just the slow spreading vines of this one anonymous shrub.

Marden walked slowly out onto the plain, half expecting he would be whistled at or scolded by someone in charge. A few pilgrims were out ahead of him, picking over the debris, acting curious and cautious at the same time. When he came up to them they stood pointing at a sheet of fabric furled around a broken strand of barbed wire.

"Observation balloon," one of the men said, pointing to a blue swatch of color. "Must have crashed here, poor devils."

The ground was covered with discarded tins, some puckered out like cone-shaped weeds, others embedded deep, as if they had been rolled and flattened by something heavy. The older ones were rusted black, but many still had legible labels. Sardine tins, tins of marmalade, a bright yellow label reading *Fortnum and Mason,* tins of something called *Harrison's Pomade.* Marden became engrossed with these, began following them as someone follows a trail. The tins, their labels, acted as homely captions to an otherwise unfathomable illustration—the only thing he had seen so far that made any sense. The first band was more than twenty yards wide, then came a gap where there were hardly any tins, and then suddenly he was up to a new band, tins with German labels, and it wasn't more than sixty yards between the German tins and the British ones.

Tins. But not only tins. There were rags and buttons and chicken bones and soggy canvas buckets and razors and tobacco pouches and pages from pay books and dirty wads of money and pictures of music hall stars and punctured canteens and corrugated iron sheeting and empty cognac bottles and soles off hobnailed boots and shredded haversacks and flypaper and rum jars and cooking dixies and a legless wicker chair and telegraph wire and broken insulators and bits of harness and end-less piles of four-by-twos, and in and around all these things, like a kind of dusting, the bright golden casings of machine gun bullets the shape and thickness of stubby pens.

The garbage lay thickest in the deepest furrows, and so it took Marden longer than it should have to under-stand these had been trenches. Most had collapsed, their lips sliding down, so they weren't much deeper than a slit dug for a latrine. Amid all of this, staring intently down, he found only one thing besides the bullet cas-ings that remained intact: a loving cup, the kind a run-ner would win at a meet. It was heavy, solid, the brass still shiny, though there was no inscription. For a moment he considered keeping it, then, thinking better of it, placed it down on the perfectly round table formed by a tree's severed stump.

Beside one of these furrows, sunken in the mud the same way as the tins, was a white marble plinth, with lettering engraved deep enough on the side that the let-ters were hidden inside their own shadows. *Be it Known you who Pass here. The Royal Welsh Fusilliers held this Trench at the First Battle of Ypres October 1914. The Royal Welsh Fusilliers Hold this Trench still* . . . only whoever had put it up had put it up too soon. There had been a Second Battle of Ypres, a Third, a Fourth, and large pieces of the monument had been blown away, so what was left had the shape and thinness of a crescent, something you could knock down with a finger.

The trench system was so complicated here, the gouges they made so treacherous, Marden was soon forced back to the road. *Hooge,* a sign read, though there was nothing left there except what he thought at first were more tins, looking blacker and more charred than any he had seen. But this was another trick of the disorientating perspective. When he came closer, saw some pilgrims standing next to them for scale, he realized they were tanks, shattered tanks, lying sunk in the clay like it was a tank graveyard, one where the corpses were being slowly spat back to life.

Or partial life. Their treads shone greasy in the sunlight, though everything else, including the stovepipe-sized holes where the guns had been, remained caked in dirt. One tank stood on its nose as if it had tried a somersault and failed. Another lay upside-down like a helpless turtle. One of the pilgrims, a big man wearing a miner's jerkin, had his hands on one of its doors which he shook furiously, as if he wanted to do it harm.

There were thick belts of barbed wire here, most of it rusty, but some brand-new, glistening in the sunlight as if it had been coated with honey. Beneath the road were culverts, most of them smashed, so he could feel the road sag under his weight, but then came one that wasn't smashed, made of ash-colored concrete and thick iron rods. A bunker, with an entrance facing east, meaning it was German. Around it hung an astringent smell, something like iodine that jumped too urgently toward his nose. Gas? Phosgene? The reek was everywhere now, mixed in with a lighter, sweetish smell that made him think of marzipan candy.

The shattered trees looked like spikes driven deep into clay. He was used to them now, hardly gave them a second glance, but there near the limits of his seeing were smaller spikes, a forest of penny nails, arranged in a vast rectangle. People moved about these, stooped down, got back up. They were child-sized from that distance, without discernible heads, and it was a while before he realized the penny nails were grave markers, the rectangles a cemetery. In roughness, in color, it didn't look any neater than the terrain he stood on. He tried counting the nails just in the first row, then, finding it impossible from so far away, continued along the road toward the southeast.

❦

When he stopped it was at a barrier made of sandbags stretching across the last intact cobblestones. Along the top was a line of dull green helmets, the German ones round, the British ones flat, making it seem soldiers were crouched there waiting to go over the top. As it turned out, there were soldiers there, colonial troops, West Indian laborers, dressed in loose-fitting fatigues, piling duckboards into pyramids ready to burn. It was the first attempt he'd seen to clean things up, and the men, defeated by the enormity of the job, were going at it with a noticeable lack of enthusiasm.

A British sergeant had charge of them, a Lowland Scot judging by his accent, the keen wedge of his face. Marden, approaching him, was startled by a sudden fluttery blur past his head.

The sergeant laughed. "Beauty, isn't she?" He pointed to where it landed on top of a helmet. "Messenger pigeons. Abandoned here. They're lonely, with no one about. The moment they spot soldiers they come flying down, even to wog bastards like mine. Aye, and plump—notice that? The kestrels pick them off readily enough. Flying down from Norway they say. Cushy times for kestrels these are."

Marden pointed across the barricade. "According to my map there's a village called Gheluvelt straight ahead."

The sergeant hesitated. He seemed the kind of man who turned even a simple conversation into a wary negotiation.

"Well, there are numbers of people asking about G'velt today. Canadians mostly. Some asking for Passchendaele, too. Passchendaele makes this here stretch look like Princes Street Gardens."

"Yes, I've heard that. But I'm interested in Gheluvelt."

"G'velt? Why it would be worth your life to go three steps beyond the barrier here. Put it up this morning so my lads wouldn't get it in their backs. You never know when a dud will go off. You never know when—" Before he could finish there was a *whump* in the distance, then a second one that could have been its echo. The laborers hardly glanced up, but the sergeant beamed.

"What did I tell you? *Mienenwerfer*—just like giant farts! When the ground warms up the fuses go off on their own. Worth your life to take one step further. Been telling people that as they come along."

Marden, listening, felt like something was tapping him on the shoulder, tapping him hard.

"These would be mostly fathers and mothers?" he said, unconsciously mimicking the sergeant's accent.

"You would be surprised."

"Younger ones?"

"I would mean that."

"Would these be women? Young women?"

"There would be one at any rate."

"A short girl? Eighteen or nineteen? Her hair down over her forehead this far?"

"Asking for G'velt? Aye, there would be one such."

Marden looked the sergeant in the eye—he didn't want any misunderstanding, not now. "Would she be expecting a child?"

"Wearing a long overcoat. But I would say she was that beneath."

Marden stared off in the distance toward the forest of penny nails, then brought his head slowly back.

"My daughter."

He said it instinctively, deliberately, to cut off the sergeant's leer, but it was one of those lies that become true the moment it's uttered, so he didn't regret saying it, didn't regret that at all. And it worked the way he intended it to. The sergeant's manner immediately changed.

"Madness, what she's doing, sir. Strolling toward G'velt by herself like she's on picnic! It isn't just the shells either, even the gas. If it rains, there's the mud. More drowned than got shot—they kept that out of the papers, but it's true. There's disease out there, lying in pockets ready to burst. Men, too. Deserters—they're liable to do anything, seeing a young girl like that." He shook his head, pursed his lips. "She seemed the determined kind. Had her hands balled up in little fists, and her eyes . . . Well, you know yourself, sir, I can see you're the same kind. She came right up to me, like she was going to knock me down if I got in her way, so I told her about another way to go, down around by Zandvoorde. It's long, but it's her only chance, which is what I said to her just like I'm telling you."

"What time was that?"

"We'd hardly gotten to work here. But she's walking slowly, the way of a girl who's in that way. You might still catch her if you're quick. There's a communication trench loops off the road back by those tanks."

XX

He gave me my instructions and I started out, nearly running in order to catch up to what my heart was doing. It raced hard with what he told me. The turn he mentioned was back toward Hooge, a trench hardly deeper than a thumb scratch in the clay. There were shell holes, so I had to do some climbing, both up and down, and that got my heart racing even more. The debris here was thicker than any spot I'd seen, so my idea of catching her was simply not in the cards. At one point I thought I saw her footsteps, but when I got closer I saw they were a mule's—petrified, seven or eight in a row, then suddenly nothing, making it seem the mule, with one last skipping bound, had taken to the air.

The communication trench led into a deeper trench back onto a lonely road, and, with the sun going down now, it was hard knowing where I stood in relation to Ypres. The debris is so extensive, blown to such uniform bits, it makes it seem a giant machine or harrow, a *single* machine or harrow, has combed through the land and passed on . . . Finally admitted to myself I was lost. Worse than lost. Felt like I was embarked on a race, a blind man's bluff, and didn't know where the finish line was. Stupid of me, worse than stupid. Why can't I sense Billy more surely now that I'm so close? Why is this girl's instinct toward him so much more certain, to the point where at every step of the way she's one march ahead? Why do her three days with him trump my eighteen years? Tried calling her name, there at the last little rise—thought by yelling, my voice might catch her. Fat chance that. Nothing human can survive this wretched landscape, not a puny weak voice like mine, nothing in the silence but the distant cooing of doves—that and the high thin whistle of the kestrels picking them off.

A bad moment. The worst so far. Terrible sense of solitude, terrible longing for Laura. Her instinct would be surer than mine. Her instinct would match the girl's.

Something odd happened now—as if anything could be other than odd here. Staring toward the east, my eyes needing something to fix on, I saw a man's bent shape, a man bending and stooping, picking things up, putting them back down again, walking slowly onward, disappearing below the furrows where they fell, reappearing where they rose high again, everything in his posture, his actions, suggesting a man embarked on a lonely search. He was a half mile away, on the enemy side of the line, deep within the German part of the Salient. My mirror image—only I didn't need a mirror to know who it was, who he was searching for, what he felt.

That was that. I couldn't go any further. Not today. Not with what I felt there.

Returning to Ypres, I came upon the deepest trench yet. Barbed wire enclosed it on three sides, forming a barrier there was no way around except by entering past a little kiosk hammered out of salvaged duckboards. A soldier stood there accepting people's money—a dark-complexioned, tough-looking private with three wound stripes chevroned on his sleeve. Canadian, judging by his loudness, the coaxing way he called to pilgrims, got them started on a tour. The Maritimes somewhere—a fisherman or miner. He's onto a good thing, as most of the other trenches are either smashed in, flooded, or filled with debris. At least twenty pilgrims waited on line, and nearly that number walked along the bottom of the trench, pointing at things, punching their fists into the sides to see how solid, getting up on the firestep to peer gingerly over.

I got close enough to look down. It's about eight feet deep, lined with wicker revetting, clean duckboards running along the bottom, sandbags piled neatly across the lip so there are no interstices or gaps. Clean and antiseptic, a chloride of lime smell having wiped out anything foul—a model trench, the trench the manuals showed, the trench mothers and fathers pictured back at home. So, good business for the private. He saw me, made a scolding motion. "Hey, no free lookin'!" he yelled, but by then I was already on the road back to Ypres.

Found a new wave of pilgrims had arrived today. They buy their blankets, a mug of soup, search for a hole in which to spend the night. How quickly you become a veteran in these circumstances. I'm stopped every few yards, asked if I know the way to Langemarck, Polygon Wood, Hellfire Corner, the Yser Canal, Messines Ridge. On the rue des Chiens, outside M. Brunfaut's garage, the same automobiles wait to be repaired that were there this morning, only now Brunfaut himself is there—a small, terrier-like man who looks like his wife.

He speaks excellent English. When I complimented him, he explained he ran the first Michelin garage in Newcastle back in 1912. He's the former mayor of Ypres, one of those jealous and intelligent men who, war or no war, keeps track of every stranger within his jurisdiction.

I mentioned Connor's name, explained why I had come, what I was searching for. He looked at me sharply before answering.

"You are seeking to actually set foot in Gheluvelt? Or are you merely trying to find information about your son?"

"Set foot there. Learn more."

"That is fine, because in either case the best solution for you is to visit the British cemetery at Zillebeke." He put his hand up. "Yes, I comprehend your dilemma.

Your boy is missing, there is no grave. But the caretaker there, Francis Cubitt, knows all there is to know about the Canadians. I advise your going to see him."

I thanked him, then, as I was leaving, asked him to give my regards to Connor next time they talked.

"How good a friend were you?" he asked, looking at me the same sharp way as before.

"We met on the boat coming over. We talked—we traveled together. We found we could understand each other very easily."

He shook his head. "Monsieur Connor died Monday afternoon in the front line near Thiepval. A shell buried in the clay went off—not near to him, very far. But as happens, it set off another shell and then another, so the explosion came toward him in a chain. I am told that he did not move, did not make the effort to take cover or run. A sad story." He shrugged his shoulders—in weariness, not irony. "*Mort pour la compagnie.*"

XXI

This was another lesson for Marden—the way you carried yourself when you got such news. He walked through the tunnel of debris, hardly glancing at it now, detouring whenever he came upon another pilgrim, dreading their questions. When he reached the wall where he had spent the previous night he found a woman had moved in, with a boy who must have been ten or eleven, the first child he had seen. He was a fine-looking boy, with quick blue eyes—like any alert, intelligent boy with his future all before him. Was his mother bringing him there to see his father's grave? Bringing him because, having lost her husband, she was taking no chances with her son? This was cruel of her, he decided, then quickly changed his mind. No, it was better that way. Let them all come, see for themselves the Salient that had taken their fathers.

Both the woman and the boy seemed very concerned about depriving him of his place, but he assured them he would find another. Rolling up his blanket, he set out along the outside of the wall, making for the Menin Road again, not stopping until forced to by darkness.

The shell hole he spent the night in was on the edge of No Man's Land, slurred into the level of the general barrenness. There were plenty of holes closer to Ypres, but he was trying to shake off the feeling that had dogged him all day, the sense he was a slacker, a coward, not fit for the job at hand. Many times during the war he had felt like that, sought solace in long walks along the rocky headlands, concocting wild, impotent schemes about joining up. But the feeling was more intense now that the test, the gauge of courage, lay so much closer. That was the reason for coming here, one of them anyway—to try his luck out in the open, not cowering behind a wall. The second reason was simpler. Here, east of the city, he was nearer his son.

The hole was shallow, grooved, giving the impression of a shell that had gone skipping along the surface rather than plunging in deep. Around the edges were new specimens of debris. Bully beef tins, torn strips of canvas, splintered stretcher poles, what looked to be the mangled insides of a gramophone. As shallow as it was, the hole and its lip of garbage offered at least some protection from the wind. It blew with more force now, as the clouds rolled themselves in the steely scent of rain.

He wrapped his blanket around his shoulders, lay on a slant so his head came over the crater's lip. It surprised him that eyes could adjust to such blackness, and yet, after that first half hour of peering, he found he could see surprising amounts of detail. The shiny filament of wire, the way it shone silver where the strand was single, brass where it lay in coils. The iron pickets pinning it down. The shattered trees with their gaping cavities, their abrupt severed limbs. Past these was a luminous band of yellow-blue, pulsing in louvered shafts like the searching beams from someone's lantern. Gas effects? Subterranean fires? It was impossible to say.

The wind grew strong enough to bring to life many things that until now had been silent, creating a raking kind of noise, as if the debris were being winnowed and sifted. Within this came a high insistent tinkling, like canteens being rattled by those needing water, and then something softer, more urgent, the guttural sound boys might make whispering to each other trying not to be heard.

It frightened him—the whispering, the yellow light, the explosions that came with increasing frequency as the night turned damp. He remembered reading about shellshock, how even the bravest soldiers would succumb to it in the end, their nerves used up, and here his nerve was finished after being in the Salient little more than twenty-four hours. His body shivered with it, his heart pounded against the ground as if digging its own funk hole, his head jerked down for cover at even the slightest new sound. If he had come this far to find out whether he had the courage to go further he had his answer now—it was a test he failed. This was the edge of where he could push himself. To go further, to go, as the boys had gone, over the top into darkness, was impossible.

Old man. He said the words out loud, as if there were someone lying in the shell hole next to him he must make his confession to at once. *Old man.*

If he still peered intently into the darkness, tried making sense of what he saw, it was little more than superstition on his part, the feeling that if he didn't stand sentry this way then his last hostage to fortune, Elaine Reed, would somehow come to harm. Superstition—recourse of the helpless. On the evening when Billy had left for war, taking the boat to the mainland . . . after the strained attempts at joviality at the pier, the few inadequate words telling him how much they loved him . . . after all this, when he and Laura returned to the house, Laura had lit a kerosene lantern in the kitchen window facing the strait, hoping Billy would see it from the ferry as it steamed eastward, take it to represent all they couldn't tell him in words.

It became her superstition, lighting the lamp every night, even during storms—only as the war went on, her routine became more complicated. Not only must the lamp be lit, it must be lit at a certain time, the wick trimmed to a certain height, and, what's more, she had to touch certain things before she touched the lamp itself—the curtains, the back of the rocker, the old brass spyglass, the cradle used now to hold her sketches—so it required a half hour or more for the ceremony to be completed, fate assuaged for another night. Foolish of her, he thought, looking on. Hopeless, lonely, tragic. And yet, once she was gone, when there was no one left to light the lamp in precisely the right way, Billy had died.

And now it was his turn to be superstitious—to feel that if he closed his eyes for even a second it would spell destruction for Elaine Reed. She was out there somewhere, he was certain of it—somewhere much closer to Billy than he was himself. So he watched, fighting off sleep, with no warmth beside the sodden blanket. Out over No Man's Land, triggered by who knew what, an unexploded flare became agitated enough to leave its casing and arc skyward, smearing its green against the underside of a cloud, cooling into a perfect yellow petal, drooping earthwards as below it, rising up on all sides, came the appreciative yipping of dogs.

XXII

The next day was the last in Marden's journey. It opened with a steady rain dropping from clouds shaped like saucers that had been tipped upside-down, mirroring the shell holes. The rain turned tea-colored as it fell, darkened by dust rising under the drops' weight. The entire landscape gave this effect—of leaping toward the rain, welcoming it, yearning to be flooded. Marden felt tempted to strike out cross country, but lakes were forming everywhere, extending fingers toward each other, broadening, so he had to keep on the long way instead, taking advantage of the height offered by the cobbled road, slick as it was. Four hours it took him, with detours. Four hours walking a compass distance of two miles.

Zillebeke cemetery, once he got there, consisted of row after row of simple wooden stakes crossed by smaller stakes. Some had circles nailed to the back of the cross—the Catholics, the boys from Ireland, the Sullivans and O'Connors. Wooden wedges with numbers had been hammered into the ground along each row for purposes of orientation. Weeds grew around the base of these, with here and there the tentative beginnings of a vine. The ground between crosses was the same drab clay as elsewhere, only attempts had been made to roll it smooth; compared to the rest of the battlefield it seemed like a garden.

Names were engraved on the crosspieces, blackened deep as if with burning irons. One cross, much larger than the others, touched crosspieces with a similar cross, forming the cemetery's entrance. A concrete urn, horribly ugly, sat beneath it, and the rain was heavy enough now that a gray cascade poured over its lip.

Marden, penetrating deeper along the duckboard paths, saw that some of the crosses had already been decorated. Crucifixes, rosary beads, bits of ribbon, here and there a small flag. One cross had a photograph nailed to its center—a boy, a boy's mustache, a boy's bashful grin, all of it turned old and wrinkled in the rain. Each square of graves had twenty rows. Each row had fifty crosses. It was flat enough he could see ten squares. Ten thousand graves. Fourteen cemeteries in this part of the Salient alone . . . but that was enough multiplication for him, and with a violent turning gesture he continued on.

There were no visitors besides him. At the cemetery's

edge lay a steam saw, the kind he remembered from logging days, and beside it a high pile of unseasoned wood that looked to be ash. To one side of it, down on his hands and knees, a man patted and scooped at the earth. Catching sight of Marden, he stood up, wiped his hands off, started over via the duckboards, making a knight's move to thread the squares.

"Morning, sir!" he called, when he was still ten rows away.

He was a rotund, pleasant-looking man in a khaki uniform, over which he had thrown a shepherd's coat with the fur turned the wrong way out. Something about him—the pipe he smoked, the rosy impetigo of his cheeks, the spectacles that perched on his nose—gave him an air of patient benevolence, so it was obvious from that first glimpse that the authorities, searching for a caretaker, had found the perfect man.

"Foul day," he said, puffing hard on the pipe.

Marden nodded. "Foul day."

The caretaker made a sweeping motion with his hand. "All temporary of course. Raw, the crosses are. We'll have them marble before very long. And the gardens. Come spring, we'll do the planting. Roses, forget-me-nots, primrose. I tell that to everyone who comes. That it will all be lovely in the end. As beautiful as it was when we first came over."

"You were here yourself?" Marden asked.

The caretaker nodded. "Special gas brigade, Royal Engineers. Three years straight without leave. Oh, I had my leave, but I let my mates take it. Feel the same way now. Everyone in such a hurry to get back to Blighty, and yet I couldn't leave. I'd up and say that to the lads. How can you leave, knowing what went on here, with your friends all lying out there in the mud? How can you just up and leave? They didn't catch my drift. Thought I was mad. But when I heard about the chance to be caretaker, I hopped at it straight away."

He stuck out his hand. "Francis Cubitt."

"Charles Marden."

There was a weed just below them Cubitt didn't like the look of. He stooped down to pluck it, placed the stem carefully in his pocket.

"Now, sir. Not many visitors about, you're only our second one today, so I can help you personally. Who is it you're looking for? If you give me your son's name and regiment and identification number we can look him up in our register quick as that."

"I'm looking for my daughter."

It all but choked him to say it, the throb that raced through his heart, the sweet lonely feeling. Cubitt was a smart and sensitive man, and yet he read it wrong, at least to start with.

"All soldiers resting here, sir. The nurses would be over at Mousetrap Farm, the few who perished."

"She's looking to find where her fiancé died. Her lover. A small woman, young. She would have asked you for help—for directions. She's expecting a child."

Cubitt's pipe, the stem, went stiff in his mouth. "Right then," he said, yanking it out. "Follow me."

He led the way through the rows until they reached the cemetery's furthest corner, to a Nissen hut with a faded red cross painted on the side. It was cozier than it looked to be from the outside. There were ammunition boxes for chairs, a cast iron stove, a boiling pot of tea.

Cubitt fussed with getting it ready, added condensed milk and sugar, handed the mug over on a souvenir tray of Brighton. It rained harder now, enough to rattle the metal roof, and Cubitt had to raise his voice to be heard.

Earlier this morning when he first left his tent, he explained. A small figure walking in through the entrance, like the wind had blown her there from the trenches. What's the word? Forlorn? A forlorn little shape, her coat bulging out in front of her so it was obvious about her condition . . . Looking for a boy named William Marden, Canadian Division, Princess Alexandra's regiment, missing near Gheluvelt . . . He led her over to the testimonial to the unknowns, the missings, or where it would one day be at any rate, but she wasn't satisfied with that, the unknown part, kept insisting she wanted to find the exact place he had gone down . . . Her story came out after returning to the hut, the poor shivering thing. It was like her pluck had carried her this far, but now she couldn't go on alone. Talked fast the way someone will who hasn't talked for a long time . . . The boat to Calais, walking to Poperinghe, walking into Ypres, spending nights living in shell holes, the terrible sounds, the shadows, the explosions, hardly anything for food . . . She'd gotten his name from Martin Peters at St. Jan, the caretaker there . . . Shivering now, so he gave her a sweater, told her to keep it, kept filling her mug with tea . . . She wanted to know about the Princess Alexandras, where they were in the line during October's fighting. She had asked at their headquarters back in Blighty, but they gave her the runaround, told

her the regiment had never been near any such place
. . . He quickly set her straight on that. The Andras had
been there all right, big trench raid just before the October advance. Poor officers by this stage, the first batch
having been killed, the new batch second-raters, and all
in all it had been a bad show. They'd not gone over, the
bulk of the lads. Mutinied, though no one would use
the word. That's why they denied it back in England. A
blot on the regiment's record, after fighting well for so
long.

"G'velt? Why yes, sir, I could have told her how to
get there, but it's impossible. The ground won't be
cleared for months yet. You can't go fifty yards without
setting off some shells, even a slip of a girl like her.
Besides, she wants to see the exact spot, and I couldn't
give that to her, though I know a man who can."

As carefully as Marden listened, his reactions at every
point lagged behind what Cubitt was telling him.
"What was she like?" he asked, once the explanation
seemed finished.

"Like? Well, pretty I must say, but needing someone
to look out for her."

"Wearing?"

"Officer's coat, not a thick one. Scarf that was just a
whisp of a thing really. Her boots—well, I offered to
find her a pair, we have so many."

"Her mood. How did she seem to you?"

"Seem? Like any girl would, losing her sweetheart.
Some come here all exhilarated like, to see the grave site.
Oh, they cry of course, but you know it's doing them a
world of good. Others become like the clay you see out
there. Cold, hard, numb. You can see it happen just

standing there looking down the way they do. Their edges start slipping away, there's no *them* anymore, if you see what I mean. No defenses. That's what you learned fast out here, what the worst thing is to be. Without defenses at all."

"And this one? Elaine?"

"Well, sir."

"Go on."

"I would say the girl has no defenses left at all."

Cubitt stood up, peered out beyond the roof's overhang toward his cemetery, unable to go five minutes without checking to see how things stood. Marden joined him there, so they stood just inside the curtain of rain.

"You said you sent her on to another man, someone who knows more?"

Cubitt nodded. "Tommy Dawson. He was in the Princess Alexandras. He was there in the raid. He can tell her the exact spot if any man can."

"How long ago was this?"

"Two hours. I expect she's chatting with him right this very minute."

"In Ypres?"

"On the G'velt side. He's a bit of a card, Tommy is. Couldn't bring himself to leave the Salient, same as me in that respect. But what he's hit upon is a scheme in a business sort of way. Has a trench he does, Piccadilly Trench. Appropriated it like. Sort of a museum for visitors, and he's charging a good fee. I sent her to see him. As mentioned, she's probably chatting with him right now."

Two hours. In the Salient, trying to make time, it was a substantial lead. And yet Marden felt steadier now than he had felt for days, his impatience finally mastered. Steadiness now. Coolness. It all depended on that.

Cubitt walked him back to the entrance, holding a scrap piece of metal over their heads as an umbrella. He gave him directions to the trench, though Marden remembered it well enough. He seemed to be hesitating, then finally came out with it just before Marden started out.

"He's a different sort of bloke than I am, Tommy Dawson. You need to prepare yourself for that, sir, same as I told her. A different sort of bloke altogether."

XXIII

It took me twice as long as it should have. The rain had flooded the shell holes, some of them deep like witch's cauldrons, blackened and stained at the rims, while others were broader, shallower, like the frying pans used in logging camps, covered with a greasy-looking stew. The wind blew strong—some of the holes were large enough to have whitecaps. As the kettles filled, overflowed one into the other, the lakes grew larger all the time, and the only peninsulas left were all mud. I'd never seen mud like that before. Thick, glutinous, greedy. Turd-colored, pus-colored, scum-colored—there are no words foul enough to do it justice. I stuck to the road, but the road was bad enough, with mud writhing across it in snake-like mounds. It was starting to get dark out, though it was hardly three yet, night coming early on account of the storm.

Dawson's trench, the trench for tourists, was still comparatively dry. I walked over to the ticket kiosk without anyone challenging me, then edged past the barbed wire and called out his name. Business was bad with the storm—there was no sign of pilgrims. Cut vertically into the wall of the trench was an oval opening. Dawson, wrapped in a trench coat, sat there with his legs crossed like an Indian, writing in what looked to be a ledger, a rum jar planted in the dirt as a kind of table. He must have seen me peering down. He made an angry dismissive gesture with his hand, like I was a fly he could simply brush away.

"Closed! Understand that? Closed!"

There was a ladder made of heavy logs—I had no trouble going down. The trench being deep like that, the wind swept much of the rain on past. Protected by the earth, walking between those vertical walls, I felt what those boys must have felt. Safe. For the time being, safe.

"Closed," Dawson said. If he'd had a grenade, he would have gladly tossed it at me. "Bugger the fuck off."

He had changed since I'd first seen him. The cockiness was gone, the handsome sense of himself. His face was the same color as his greatcoat, making it seem the olive fabric had bled into his skin. Above his left eye, angled upwards like an extra eyebrow, was a deep furrowed scar, and there was another even deeper, paler one near his opposite temple. He wore fingerless gloves of a thick brown wool, and it made his hands seem enlarged and crippled.

And he was shivering—that's the other thing I noticed. He seemed feverish, the rims of his ears were bright red, and everything he said came interrupted by a spasmodic cough.

"Well, isn't this fucking wonderful," he said, once that first fit passed. "It's Billy Marden day. Bleeding Billy Marden day right here in Piccadilly trench."

"Oh Christ, you look just like him," he said, catching sight of my expression. "A bad joke if you ask me. Fathers all looking like their sons. And besides, that girl was here asking after him already. A whole frigging parade."

He reached for the rum jar, dipped his mug in, knocked it back. There was a bench built in the dugout wall, and he surprised me by moving aside, slapping it with his hand.

"Take a load off, Mr. Marden. The attack isn't scheduled until nineteen hundred hours, giving us exactly two more hours to shiver, shit and puke."

His mood matched the rain, the storm. Maybe that was one of the tricks of survival, I decided—not to fight it, but to let everything wretched seep in. Billy had died and he had lived, and right from that first moment I was looking to find what the difference was, to discover Dawson's trick.

"Not a bad little piece, that girl of his. Being knocked up like that makes her face glow, let alone what it's done for her tits. So Billy had some fun back in England. He deserved it, the sorry bastard. Bad luck he's not around to see the results. She seems a brave sort. She wanted some information and she wasn't going to be put off."

"What did you tell her?"

"That when it comes to tours of the Salient, souvenirs, historical tidbits, I have a patent until someone smarter or stronger comes along. As patent holder, I expect to get paid."

"Cubitt says you couldn't bring yourself to leave. That you're the kind who's lost too many friends here and can't give it up."

Dawson dug his fist into the trench wall, twisted it violently until a chunk dropped away. "I'll leave. I can't wait to leave, but I'm going to be paid first for what I saw." He pulled his fist from the dirt, touched quickly his temple, shoulder, groin, hips. "None of that matters. The metal inside. What I saw matters. I'm going to be paid for what this war did to my seeing, paid by every sorry soul who happens along."

"How much?"

"Why should I go back? To die of influenza? The one good thing about Flanders, you know what it is? Plague can't live out there, the ground's too poisoned. I'll wait until the rest of the world dies off, then I'll feel right at home . . . Six pounds. All she had. But I'll tell you this. She got a hell of a lot more truth for that than six quid could buy her in England."

I took the notes out, laid them next to the jar. Dawson coughed out a laugh, made no move to pick them up, though I noticed he entered something in his account book fast enough. *The truth about Marden. Ten quid.*

Billy took to soldiering readily enough, he said. A

boyish kind of good humor. A boyish readiness to do what his superiors said. The older soldiers, the ones who'd been out there, would sneer at this, but for some reason they didn't sneer at it in Billy, and he was a favorite right from the start. Even more so later when they moved up to the line. The sergeants were a bad lot, been out there too long and some not long enough, and the boys got so they would look to Billy for their instructions, even though he was only a corporal.

They were in reserve for a week, then up to the line for two weeks, with no relief. This was early October. It rained all that time. Whole platoons came down sick, not only trench foot, but fever, and every morning another man would be found curled up dead in a funk hole with his knees stiff to his chest. It was a quiet sector immediately in front of Gheluvelt. The Germans across the way were Saxons, good ones, and all they cared about was packing up to retreat home.

A staff officer got the idea that a raid should be mounted to show the Germans there was no slackening in British resolve. It was set for just after dark. A quick burst of shelling to cut their wire, then the raiding party dashing across the eighty yards of No Man's Land to the first German trench.

The soldiers sensed the war was over, even if headquarters didn't. They refused to leave the trench. A Captain Whymark, a cowboy from Calgary, pulled his pistol on them and threatened to start shooting. One of the men shot him first with his Lee Enfield. Shot him in the groin and rolled the corpse over the lip of the trench toward the wire, so it looked liked the Germans had gotten him.

Billy took over—him and a couple of the other strong corporals. He stood in the pool of blackness at the bottom of the trench ladder, clasping and unclasping his fists like a hardened warrior, chewing his tongue like a frightened ten-year-old—and yet making sure each man got a word from him, a reassuring pat on the back as they went over.

Dawson went along, since he knew what the military police could do to those who funked it. Only the Germans must have sensed something, because the moment the raiders set off the flares started raining down, so it was bright as noon, a noon that was green. The Germans were furious at being attacked when they were retreating, so they turned and let loose with everything they had. Trench mortars, *Mienenwerfer,* machine guns, gas.

Their wire wasn't cut. Instead of sixty men to take the trench, there were only the nine of them. The wind whipped gas back in their eyes, the barrage had them straddled, so it was hell to go on, utterly useless. They started running back to their own line past the bodies of those who had already fallen. Billy ran first. There was an old pillbox behind them nicknamed the Funhouse. They ran toward the Funhouse, throwing their rifles away, like little boys racing each other to a lake ready to plunge in.

Billy, running first, got hit first. A bullet tumbled him over, then a shell did the rest. Dawson had the sight of him going down toward the mud, then blowing apart, so there was nothing, no reason to stop, no corpse to drag back, nothing you could even shovel into a sandbag. Two men returned to the trench alive, Dawson and a private named Jenkins, another cowboy, this one from Regina.

Dawson's words trailed off the way words will when they're not strong enough anymore, not simple enough, to stand against what they're saying—trailed off like someone's confession will when they stand before you in the dock. Above the trench, the wind blew harder, making a sound like an express train barreling along ice-grooved tracks. The rain had collapsed part of the revetting. Dawson, cursing, jumped up to fix it. When he did, I noticed he had a rifle next to him, a puttee wrapped around the barrel to keep it dry. He took it with him. He wouldn't move in that trench without taking his gun.

He pressed a match to a lantern, stood there at the end of the traverse with a spade, digging away in the yellow beams. His repairs gave me time to try and catch up. Here he thought that by being cynical, truthful, he would blast me away, and not only me, but who I represented, all the uncaring civilians he hated, even as he took their cash. And yet he had told me something vital—that part about Billy and his squad running past the pillbox like boys splashing into a lake.

We were on a pack trip to the north of the island, the late summer of 1912. Laura was shy of her painting, but she was good at it, and had gone off to sketch while I tried my luck in one of the high alpine lakes. I stood casting toward rising trout I couldn't quite reach, when I heard shouts behind me, laughter, and around the nearest clump of pine appeared Billy and his mob, the friends he spent all summer with, Billy their leader, and they raced past me, breaking apart the meadow grass, and dove brown and naked into the shallows.

I remember how beautiful they looked—in that wonderland of mountains and meadows and wildflowers, they in their muscled grace were the most beautiful sight, their arms extended, reaching, the alternate rhythms of their strong tanned shoulders, the delicate little sips of air they took as their heads rolled clear.

Billy swam furthest and surfaced last, not ten yards from where I stood trying to fool those trout. "Oh hello, Dad," he said, tilting his head the way he did, smiling, surprised, delighted with himself, with his friends, with the mountains, with me . . . And I thought, remembering this, thought so fiercely it made my heart throb into my throat, that one day this will all happen again . . . that we shall come someday, Laura and I, to the place where he stands waiting in a high alpine lake. He will see us. "Hello, Dad," he will call. He will ask after the fishing. I will smile, get over my shyness, reach out for him. I will feel the grip of his young, strong arms about me just as in the happy days before that day which is of all the days in my life the most terrible and hateful.

Billy ran. In war, given responsibility, the enemy before him, he turned and ran. I knew what I was supposed to feel over this, what the colonels wanted me to feel, the generals, the politicians, those in charge of sending boys to their destruction. Embarrassment, mortification, shame. But I felt none of those things. I felt glad for him. Glad that in the last moment of his life, facing that unstoppable machine with its mincing harrow, he became a boy again, did what any boy would

do, run with all his strength toward life, toward safety
. . . and my only regret, the regret that will never heal, is
that he did not run faster.

The spade cutting the earth. The hissing sound of the
lantern. The wet, concussive roar overhead. The blackness. The frightened contractions of my heart. These are
my memories now, what I will live with.

Dawson came back again, his greatcoat caked in
mud, the rain on his forehead making livid his scars.
Something in the sound must have worried him, for the
puttee was off the rifle now, and his expression was
focused and wary.

He squatted down near the rum jar, seemed surprised
I was still there.

"Is this the same story you told the girl?" I asked.

He shrugged, pulled his collar up around his neck.
"She wanted the exact spot. How to get there. I had her
money so I told her. Walk east from the trench, direct
into the wind. There's a scoop in the ground, assembly
trench, and you follow that, not the road. You know
when you're getting close when you come to two tanks
in the mud. They're up on end leaning against each
other—the praying tanks we called them. That was our
advanced front line. The wire is thick, three belts where
it's not cut. Out in front is the Funhouse and eighty
yards beyond that is the German trench with more wire.
It's in between where he got hit."

He had a coughing fit, waved me away when I moved
to help him. "I know what you're thinking," he said,
though I thought nothing. "Why did I let her go? Why
didn't I stop her? Easy. She didn't want to be stopped.
She came all the way from England to find where he was

killed, but it runs deeper than that. She doesn't just want to see where he died, she wants to die there herself."

I must have grimaced here, flinched, something tangible enough to make him talk faster.

"What's the surprise in that? What kind of future does she have back home alone? You think they'll give her his pension? Not a fucking chance—there's no proof the baby is his. Her proper Brit family won't have anything to do with her. No man will marry her, not with a brat to care for. No men her age left anyway. A bastard—the kid's life won't be easy. Cannon fodder for the next war."

"And you understand all this from the ten minutes she spent here?"

"I saw that look a thousand times. You got so you recognized it. A man who had given up, wanted only to get it over with. They went over the top with their arms wide apart like this, just begging for a bullet . . . But you're right, it took me by surprise. Never saw it in a woman before. But the look in her was stronger than in anyone I ever saw. And that's saying plenty."

"You read her eyes."

"She up and told me. I gave her the directions, she thanked me like I had just given her a sweet. A polite girl—she didn't forget that, to be polite. I gave her a coat to replace the rag she was wearing. Gave her a torch to light her way. That's when she said it—by way of being polite, and because just once it had to be said out loud. 'I've come to die where he died.' You fool, I had time to think. You barmy fool. A second after that she was off."

There was a thud in the distance audible even over the wind. A moment later came a matching thud in the trench wall strong enough to tilt me forward. "French seventy-five," Dawson said. Above us, across the vertical slot of blackness framed by the sandbags, the rain swept past in green-silver streaks, like wormy little serpents.

Dawson jerked his thumb. "Here, come up here."

We stood on the firing step, our bellies tight against the dirt, our heads not quite level with the lip of the trench. I tried peering over, though with the wind that strong, the rain, it was impossible to even squint. Dawson, I noticed, couldn't do that or wouldn't do that—put his head even one inch above the trench. He smiled, seeing that I did. He put his finger to his head, bored in on his temple.

"The good thing is that you wouldn't have felt a thing."

He turned so his back rested on the trench wall, slanting backwards. He lit a Woodbine, being careful to shield the glow with his hand.

"Worse now than it was then, you know that? No one to help. No mates to come and fetch you. No stretcher bearers. No friendly trench to retreat to. As dangerous to come back as to go forward . . . The sappers planted eighteen mines under the German lines last spring. Thirteen went off, five didn't. Five mines waiting for a night like this to explode."

"I've heard stories of deserters. Organized gangs."

"Bullshit. The peasants started rumors to keep squatters from moving in on their land. Belgians stand to do pretty well by this war. They'll put in for reparations from the Germans and the English and the French, and then they'll move back and make a fortune selling scrap metal, and when that's gone they'll plant beets on the bodies, get a bumper crop their first year . . . It doesn't need us anymore. The battlefield doesn't need soldiers. There's enough ammunition out there it can spend a century fighting itself . . . And there's not a single person alive. You can be more alone out there than anywhere in the world. I like that. Peering out knowing there's not a single goddam soul."

"Except the girl."

He twisted toward me, cocked the wounded eyebrow as high as it would go. "Yes, the girl. Only she's not alive now either."

There was another explosion, this one close enough it felt like a giant had clapped his hands over my ears, fisted them, driven inward with his knuckles. I ducked, twisted, all but fell. Dawson, who hadn't flinched, was vastly amused.

"Shellshock? Funking it? Self-inflicted wound? What's keeping you, Mr. Marden? If you don't believe what I'm saying, go out and have a peek for yourself. Go. Now, while the firing's let up. They won't bother you, the bullets. They've gotten used to young flesh, they won't be interested in yours. Go. What's keeping you?"

I pressed against the dirt, trying to see, seeing nothing, readying myself for the next blast.

"Go goddammit! Go!"

He slapped my leg, slapped it hard, then, when I still didn't move, reached for the rum jar, took a long swallow. The rum smoothed his cough down, almost made his voice sound kind.

"Don't worry about it, old man. A lot better men than you turned yellow."

He disappeared down the trench toward his repairs. There was the sound of his spade biting earth, then it was replaced by a splitting, cracking sound, as if the raindrops had turned into metal. What I could see over the trench's lip was a band of blackness where the mud had replaced the sky. I tried pushing myself high enough to plant my elbows on the sandbags, but my muscles refused, the muscles in my legs, which were quivering uncontrollably. I tried pushing with my arms, but they were no good either. I tried thinking of the soldiers who had been there before me, draw courage from their example, but it didn't work—all I felt there was guilt and shame. What I sensed, felt much closer to, was that other, much larger army, the invisible pilgrims in their holes, the army of the bereaved—took comfort from them, the sheer numbers, the way I fitted in there now, if nowhere else.

When my muscles finally obeyed, did the minimum reluctant pushing needed to free me of that trench, it was only because they were used to obeying a half century's worth of commands, big and little both, so they found it easier to go along with the nagging, stubborn will that had charge of them than it was to refuse. I remembered times when my arms ached from exhaustion and there was still half the orchard to prune. I remembered times when my fingers had to grasp hard my pen and sign the sentences of poor shattered men or women who had no idea what fate had done to them or why. I remembered the weight on my shoulder of Laura's coffin as we carried her up the hill from the beach . . . remembered all the impossible tasks my muscles had performed against their will, and, by concentrating, fooled them into obeying me one last time.

I left the trench, started walking the way Dawson said, straight into the wind, the force of it as sharp and clear as a dagger held to my chin.

A plank crossed the wire, but then the mud started, a strangely airy, delicate mud. My boots slipped on it, so I skated more than ran. I came upon the assembly trench almost immediately—that was the lucky thing. The bottom was lined with rotten duckboards that broke under my weight, so my shins were always ramming up against splintered edges, but it was better than taking my chances with the flooded shell holes. The rain still had that streaky green-silver color, which added a vague light. The craters, the shallow ones, had a scum of phosphorescence floating on top, which must have been gas, because there was a briny smell now, and my eyes watered with something that seemed deeper, more essential than tears.

Where the assembly trench ended the going became harder. I knew stepping the wrong way meant drowning, but which was the right way was impossible to determine. Shells went off in the distance, making an ugly tubercular sound, like the mud was coughing. It was impossible to walk toward it without slanting forward from the waist, trying to turn my body into a meek, well-meaning shape the shells would find harmless and so allow past. There were helmets lying about— even in the blackness I could see hundreds of lumpish shells—but I couldn't bring myself to put one on. The mud seemed deeper here than what I had crossed through before, hungrier, and it kept sucking down on my legs, to the point where every six or seven strides, breaking through the crust, my leading leg would plunge down to my groin, and I would have to sit down on what hummocks there were and use both hands to yank it back out.

I was into a zone of skeletons now, horse or mule skeletons, with those big leering jawbones bleached white as ivory. They looked as if they had been killed all at once, by one concentrated barrage, because they lay in a well-defined heap—souvenirs of First Ypres or Second Ypres or Fourteen Ypres or whatever the count had gone up to. At first, I made detours to get around, but then I found that by stepping on the bones I gained more purchase, so I began deliberately seeking out the dead mules as a path.

Straight ahead came the sound of exploding shells, rapidly, like a huge chain that flailed away from me. Away from me, I was sure of it, but just when I relaxed from my crouch, breathed easier, something took me and rolled me over, rolled me over again, the way heavy surf does, with negligent, absentminded malice. I stumbled to my feet, but immediately came a crueler shove right between the shoulder blades that hurled me face first into the mud. It yielded beneath me, so within seconds I was below the rim of the earth. I wasn't frightened by this, not in the usual way of fear, but I was completely unable to move, other than the frantic twitching, the uncontrollable spasms, my legs made on their own. I felt detached, apart from myself, curious to see how far

I would sink, how willingly the earth would yield to me, how close and snug it would shape itself to my body before swallowing me whole.

Here is how they drowned—the one thought I held clear. I felt a childish uncertainty, wanting to know if I was all right, needing an adult to tell me so, since I was no longer responsible for my own safety. My leg, sinking, brushed against something sharp enough to scratch me, and this is what revulsed me most—the ugly tickle of that machine-cold metal on my skin. I kicked, swam with my hands, fought my way back up. There was a broken piece of duckboard; I wallowed toward it like it was a raft, sat there to catch my breath again, slapped at the mud until it dropped in cakes from my legs and hips, looked around again, started off.

As before, I did best on the pathway formed by bones. They were smaller here, more numerous, without the ivory luminescence the first ones had, and they lay in jackstraws pointing a hundred directions at once. I felt stupid, walking across them. Stupid in a way there is no measure for. I didn't know there were so many mules in the front line. So many small mules. So many small, sorry mules in the world.

I dropped into a communication trench again, or maybe it was an assembly trench or a second-line trench or a traverse or a sap. There were too many gouges in the earth to give them all names. Along the bottom, following the declination eastward, flowed a regular river, carrying on its froth pieces of wood, wire and tin. It stayed deep enough, strong enough, to push on my legs, while, higher, the wind lashed my face. Gas had ignited here, despite the rain—it burned in little cups of blue flame, like a thousand burners, making it easier to see. Directly ahead of me rose Dawson's praying tanks, upended, so their treads, the part of them that resembled paws, rubbed right against each other, as if they were locked in combat over a mate.

Framed in the center was a yellow pinprick of light. I knew what it was, what it had to be: a torch, the torch Dawson had given her. "Elaine!" I yelled, but the gas had dried my throat up, and no sound emerged, or no sound that could penetrate the wind.

I started toward her, wondering if I was imagining things—the yellow immediately disappeared. The arch formed by the tanks kept the rain off, and it was tempting to stay there, the treads hovering protectively over my head. Just beyond sat a flat concrete surface that was absurdly smooth compared to anything else I had stumbled upon, like a floor plopped down there so the boys could dance. Was it the Funhouse? It could have been. There were iron hoops embedded in the top for strength, narrow loopholes cut for guns. It *must* have been—and yet it was sinking in the mud, all but swallowed, to the point I could feel it subside beneath my weight.

This was where Billy had died. I waded to the left, northwards, to make sure, then stood there on what seemed, in its pointed solitude, the last dry hummock left in the world. I closed my eyes, tried concentrating. This was the place Billy had ceased—and ceased forever—to be Billy. I told myself this, and yet my mind could not get around it, couldn't wrestle the words into anything that made sense. There was a soggy scratching noise, a long sibilant hiss, and then a flare arced through the sky and burst straight overhead. It cast the same greenish light the storm carried, but intensified, heated, so for the thirty seconds it took to fall to earth it blazed bright as day.

A hundred yards away, small against the rolled crust of a crater, framed by the black tusks of shattered trees, stood the girl. She had on Dawson's coat, it covered her like a mustard-colored cape, and yet there was something so essentially feminine about her silhouette there could be no mistake. She was frozen in the posture the landscape demanded, slanting forward to let the horror sweep past. It conveyed bravery, not despair—in that first glance I felt a wild, giddy surge of hope. She turned in my direction, made a sweeping motion with her hand as if to push the coat back from her eyes, then, the light drowning in the rain, turned and began hurrying away.

I frightened her—my black and looming silhouette against the garish light. I tried yelling again, but it was useless. I forced myself back into the mud for another twenty yards, then felt something tighten around my middle, a sharp pointy jab in the small of my back. It yielded far enough to permit another full step, then, coming taut again, snapped me back so violently I almost fell.

Wire. Barbed wire, which until then I'd only seen in loose rusty coils, no more troubling than briars or thorns. Here were entire belts of it, intact, solidly anchored by iron pickets. It held me by a dozen points at once, so when I pulled in one direction, it tightened in another, and always with that sharp inward stab. My coat offered some protection, that was the good thing. By rolling sideways I was able to make progress toward the north, aslant the storm, but there was no possible way to move forward or back.

From what I could see these belts went on forever. Was the girl caught as well? I was tangled in the thickest part of the coils, pinned, unable to move; I felt a hard tug that snapped the wire forward, then another tug, then a third, making it seem as if something were trapped further along and was surging desperately to get free.

I managed to shake myself loose, stood on the muddy promontory that led between belts, lost now, dizzy. In the darkness, that driving rain, there was only one way to continue without falling into a shell hole, and that was by grabbing the wire with my hands, using it as a guide, a lifeline. I grabbed on and immediately let go— grabbed a second time, harder. The barbs penetrated my skin and ripped it, stung as if the wire were coated in salt, but I had to hold on, pressing through the pain, not losing contact, starting along the wire hand over hand. Every few feet my palms would hit something leathery and soft impaled on the barbs, something that softened the sting and yet hurt much worse, something I wouldn't let myself think about . . . and forcing this away from me, biting back the pain, I kept on, closing in on the frantic tugging on the wire that had never stopped.

I counted the barbs. I counted the barbs and the fleshy tufts caught on the barbs, and when I got to sixty-seven I reached Elaine Reed.

The wire held her as it had held me, only it coiled higher on her, seemed crueler, so her arms were pinned behind her and her neck was forced back. The torch

Dawson had given her lay at her feet, a little stick of yellow pointing upwards. I could see her face above the greatcoat's collar, or a flash of it, the same kind of glimpse I'd had of her picture back at her parents'. Large eyes, delicate forehead, long hair—all made wild and exaggerated by the rain and the dark. The wire, coming taut, turned her in my direction and swept back her hood . . . turned her, that is, toward a hulking shape coming at her from where the blackness lay thickest.

She seemed—posed there. Immobile. Still. Time had to stop, the unsparing rush of it, in order to allow us to complete its utter defiance. Even the slightest movement would have made time snap back with a vengeance and carry us away. The silhouette so balanced between girl and woman, the slightness, the fullness, the tattered open coat. One second. Two seconds . . .

Making a last convulsive effort, she broke free of the wire—broke free, but instead of running away came *toward* me, toward me like those frightened pigeons lost on the battlefield, desperate from loneliness. And yet the effort must have exhausted her, because before she could reach me, she sank to her knees, was on the point of toppling face first into the mud, when I reached her, caught her, pulled her to my side.

The gas scratched my throat, I couldn't talk, but maybe it was better I couldn't, better that whatever I had to convey to her, convey to her immediately, came through my arms. I felt her struggle against me, into me. Our hands found each other's and clasped hard. Even shivering the way she was, sodden, coated with mud, I could feel the warmth that lay at her core. I could feel her heart—it beat so fast, so strong, it could have been two hearts, with mine making the third. I picked her up so I could carry her in my arms, felt her arms come around my neck. She shuddered one more time before lying still in a way she must have sensed would help me—a convulsive shudder that came from the deepest part of her, not in revulsion at the horror, but in a reflex, a judgement, toward life.

There were no words to answer this, no need for words. Who I was, why I had come for her, how I had found her—all this was too huge to explain, and so I said nothing. Safety for her lay in staying near me, and safety for me was holding close that vital throb in her, that instinct toward life, the human smell, the wisps of her hair, the sound of her breathing, the fullness of what she carried. I let her down now; I held onto her like a life ring, she used me like a cane, and together we made it to the Funhouse, stood on its sinking firmness staring wildly about. Her hands were cold, they were clenched into fists inside mine, and whatever had to be said between us came in the communication of those bunched fists, those interwoven knots there was now no possibility of severing.

Before us was a hole as dark and round as a mine entrance, and from it came an updraft of foul-smelling air that chilled us, blew back our hoods. I helped her around the edge, kicking with my boots to make sure of the footing. Past this came a sharp tangle of steel there was no identifying, and this time it was she who found the way around. This was something, these were our baby steps, we were learning to trust each other, but they took us nowhere, did nothing to lessen the vastness of that dark. I knew we must keep moving and yet not move wrong, and for a moment the impossibility of this kept us frozen.

Flares went up behind us, the color seemed to spread down over her tattered coat, bleed into mine, so color, too, seemed trying to make us one. I turned around with her, turned around again, attempting to understand where I was, what I must do now. The wire ran in endless belts, the shell holes were everywhere, there was no glimmer of light save what was cast by poison gas. I sensed that if I headed west and walked simply, *simply,* holding her close to me, we might thread the worst of it and be safe. There was a narrow promontory, a knife edge where the mud didn't seem so bad, and there would be duckboards further along—shaky, broken, flooded, but a paradise compared to where we were now.

A knife edge, a high wire, a plank. An old man carrying an exhausted woman, pressing between us the heartbeat of a child. Fine, those were the odds, that was the task set for us. And as for which direction west lay, that was my lodestone, the sunset, the tug of it, the one thing in life I could always find by heart.